ENRICO

THE CONTI CRIME FAMILY
BOOK 3

C.M. STEELE

The Steele Press

INTRODUCTION

Enrico

She wasn't supposed to be on my radar. Another woman who was caught up in the traffickers' sights, but one look at January and I'd become as lost as Dario and Alessio before me. I had no choice but to hunt her down and make her mine, even if that meant doing some illegal things. Nothing new to me anyway.

January

The brute. I spotted him and knew he was trouble, but deep down, I hadn't expected to crave his crazy. Trying to flee a dangerous situation, I jumped right into another. The brute had me captive, and I had no choice but to trust him because someone was after me. I desired his insanity even as I pushed him to get away. Should I flee and risk running into danger, or should I stay and endanger my heart and soul?

CHAPTER ONE

ENRICO

As much as I like June, I've been annoyed with Alessio's lack of focus on delicate matters. He's so lost in his own little bubble, chasing all the men away from her and monitoring her movements that it's pissing me off. Hell, the fact that the boss hasn't been much better has stressed me out as well.

I've had to handle two issues this week that could have gone south if I'd waited for them to pull their heads out of their asses. Unfortunately, it doesn't look like it's going to happen any time soon.

Women ruin your focus, and they could get us killed. Not that I would know because I don't give women attention. My life has been too violent and rough to allow a woman into it.

Alessio and the boss are thinking with the wrong head. I wouldn't be caught falling on my ass for a woman, but I'm not letting them go down, so I pick up the slack and follow their lead.

"Dario, there are two other tenants that live on the third floor, but they are an old couple in their seventies," Alessio says as we prepare to visit Randall Johnson, who is May and June Beaman's landlord.

He's shown May too much attention, and Dario doesn't appreciate it. It's that shit I find crazy, but whatever. If he considers it disrespect, then I'm there to make the fucker more respectful, even if that silences the bastard forever.

"Good. They won't be a problem. I'm betting they'll be asleep by the time we arrive."

"Shit, they were probably asleep two hours ago," I say, thinking about my nonno, who would be out before the show he loved would come on. I had to record it so he didn't miss it.

"Hey, don't talk too much shit, Enrico. You'll be old one day, napping at noon."

"Fuck, I don't mind napping. I just know my nonno was out on the recliner by seven every night." I miss him. It's been years since he some sick fuck killed him, but I remember all the good years I had with him.

Every time I think about my nonno, I want to tear apart the bastards who came to his home that night, but it's hard to do that to scattered ashes. I butchered all those who were complicit and then destroyed their remains.

"I get it." Someone's a little on edge over his woman. "Now, let's move. I want this handled tonight because I have other plans." Of course he does, and she's the reason we're here in the first place. I'm more anxious than edgy.

Dealing with Johnson will be nothing and even a simple day's work. Men like him are a dime a dozen, but I'm just ready to get this over with.

There's a strange tension in my bones, so I roll my head and crack my neck.

"You cool," Vito asks, noticing my actions.

"Yeah, we need to get this shit over with because it's interfering with business." He chuckles and tilting his head downward to fight the laugh.

I can't explain the feeling that's been in my head all day, but it lingers there as if there's something coming and I have no idea what it is. Maybe it's the weird feeling I had the last time I was at the apartment. It felt like someone was watching me, but I didn't notice anyone.

We hop into two blacked-out vehicles, turn off all tracking devices, as always, and make our approach to Jefferson Park. Vito and two others are there for clean up while Dario, Alessio, and I were riding in the other vehicle about to make a mess.

Once we reach her block, we dip off to a side street out of the way of prying eyes and into an alley. The street is quiet even though there are a couple of crackheads buzzing about around the corner.

Still, we sneak in, popping the shitty lock to the side gate leading to the gangway and the back of the apartment building. The backyard is nothing but broken concrete with weeds coming up from under it and junk parts lying around. It's clear the women don't use the area for entertaining and probably aren't even allowed back here.

A low growl emanates from each of us. Fuck—we need to maintain control before we draw attention to ourselves. We needed complete darkness, which is perfect because the moon isn't full tonight, giving us the ability to sneak into the area unnoticed. Still, Dario tosses us a warning look and then we slink in the back way, easily opening the door to the main floor.

The sound of the television plays as we move closer to his apartment door. I have the key that Luca made when we went spying earlier in the day. Skills, the man has them in spades, and he easily made a copy for us. Once we pop the door open, we are met with a startled Johnson, nearly naked on a recliner.

"Who the fuck are you?" he shouts, jumping out of his chair.

Dario is silent, anger and tension just pouring from his body, because on Johnson's fucking center monitor screen is May, walking in just a towel. It must be from earlier in the day or a previous one because she's at work right now. It doesn't matter, because it shouldn't fucking be there.

Still, it's not the only fucked-up image in front of us. There are six screens full of different women, mostly May and June from the upstairs apartment, but several others

I'm not familiar with. I can't tell when the videos were filmed, but it doesn't matter because he's already crossed a line. Although, the videos aren't the only offending content in sight.

The bastard also has photos blatantly posted on his wall; there are several on a peg board that catch my eye because of one female in particular is in every single one of them. Most of the time she's with May and June. She's a beautiful redhead with curly hair and expressive eyes. It pisses me off how she could be the object of this bastard's attention.

My mouth waters, chest constricts while my blood boils. A new feeling washes over me as I realize who she must be. She must be January.

I'm startled for a moment when Dario lets loose on this motherfucker, beating his ass for challenging him. The violent rage pouring off the boss is understandable and as I turn back to the images all around his apartment, I grow increasingly angry.

She's in the apartment with the other two girls, smiling, her long, curly red hair loose with her hand pressed to her ample chest. There's one photo that calls directly to me.

It's as if she poses for it, but we know these are stolen shots. She's smiling for the unknown camera, giggling while wearing a green shirt that brings out her eyes. January intrigues me, so much that I can't think straight. I have to know her, and I will, but until then, I need to remove her from his sight.

Without drawing attention to myself, I give it a quick tug, taking the photo off the wall and tucking it into my suit jacket pocket. Slowly, I approach Dario's bloodbath and take a look at the screens again.

My eyes darted to another screen. I seethe with rage as I stare at my woman on this bastard's computer. My woman is sitting with her legs crossed in just panties and a tee that cuts just above her belly button, a notebook in hand and a pencil between her teeth, looking absolutely fetching.

She's clearly engrossed in making notes, not expecting to be filmed. The thought of a camera in her bedroom turns me to ice. Cold as fuck, and ready for my own vengeance.

Yes, January is my woman. I've just fucking declared that shit, and it hits me like a punch in the gut. I've lost it like the other two, and I'm not in the least bit ashamed about it.

I want this bastard's head. I'm ready to stomp his head into the ground for such a violation of privacy.

"Your just deserts." Dario's fist lands before he finishes speaking. Johnson falls back, catching the edge of the chair, and lands on the floor, sending the chair clattering against a set of boxes.

They fall open, and out cascades pictures. I picked up a stack, grateful we're all wearing gloves because there are two dozen of January alone in the same apartment as the girls. The more I see, the deeper my anger grows.

And to think, I thought Dario had lost his mind. He was much more in control than I gave him credit for. In seconds, January had become mine without knowing anything about her. My depths know no bounds.

"Shit," he hisses, going for them, but Dario's on him, unable to quit beating the man.

"We need to question him," Alessio reminds him. There are more people working with this fucker for sure.

"We don't need shit from this fuck. Everything we need is around us. He's a piece-of-shit twisted fuck with a death wish. Like you don't see June here, Alessio. Tell me again that I need to hold it together, and I'll fucking pop you one." Dario's expression is barbaric, rage-fueled, and determined.

"Understood." Alessio backs up and throws his hands up in mock surrender while Dario goes back to continue his assault, kicking the dog shit out of this worthless lifeform.

"Please stop. I want to live." It seems the more he pleads, the angrier Dario gets, and I can't blame him. If Dario didn't have the right first, I would have been the one to do it with pleasure. Hell, even Alessio has the right, but he won't until it's the last thing because he's thinking straight.

Dario gets all in his face, speaking in an even tone. "Tough. You stared at my woman, touched her with your filthy hands, dared to use her for your own sick fantasies. You don't deserve anything less than death."

Dario finishes him off with a kill shot to his head. The man is done. "Go around and get everything we can with June and May's images on it as well as their roommate's compromised photos. I don't want them tied to any of this shit. Understood?"

"Of course." We all move around the room, going through all the documents while our cleanup crew waits for Dario's call. It's then that I notice something, and my temper grows beyond the regular son of a bitch I am.

I stare at the DVDs in Johnson's apartment and my thumb flexes across my knuckles, cracking them effortlessly. Holding one with January's name written on it, I crush it in my hand easily. Never have I felt such justifiable rage in my life. He lies there in a pool of his blood, and I'm pissed that I didn't get to do the honors. Dario stole that thunder from me.

This woman on his screen had been one of Johnson's unaware victims and is now my obsession. January had shown him her private areas without knowing it, and technically every man in this room has seen them as well. Although they don't seem to care that her little kitten was nearly on display. God knows what was on that video, and I don't want to see it because there will be hell to pay for anyone he could have sold that video to.

Turning around to his mutilated corpse, I whipped out a knife and staked him in the heart. "Prick."

"He had it coming," Alessio mutters when Dario stares at me in shock. It wasn't like he hadn't fucking gone buck wild on this motherfucker moments earlier. He mastered the art of psycho on this sad fuck just minutes ago. I can't believe how insane our calm boss had been, but we both saw the way he'd looked at the waitress at Coleman's diner.

May Beaman is his obsession, and Johnson had touched what didn't belong to him. Hell, I finally understood it all, and it only took a moment for me to get feel the obsession take over.

"Let's get the guys in to clean this up. I have another matter to deal with tonight. Alessio, you go home and tend to your woman. Enrico, you and Vito will be coming with me for this one." I nodded, pressing my lips shut because I had no desire to leave, but I wasn't going to argue with the madman at my side.

As we made our exit, I stole a glance upward toward the next floor where my future wife slept. She was unaware of the danger below for so long, and I'm grateful that we eliminated it before he could harm her even more.

I ached to sneak into their apartment and steal a moment alone with January, but I had to bide my time. She didn't have to sleep alone, and soon she wouldn't because I'd lay claim to her. I am certain that I'll do anything to have her as mine, even if that means snatching her up under the cover of night.

The second we're in the SUV, Dario taps my shoulder and with his voice just above a growl, he says, "Make no moves until I've gotten May under my roof, understood?" He's read me easily and I can't say I blame him for his reasoning. Getting May under his roof is essential.

"Yes, Dario."

We head out to the diner with me in the driver's seat so Dario can speak to his woman. What I'd prefer to do is question her ass all about her friend, learn everything about her, every like and dislike, find every ex-boyfriend and lover so I could fucking kill them.

Yes, I'm a damn crazy bastard, but that's why I'm Dario's enforcer. I snap necks, slice up bodies, and end lives when necessary, so it's not like I wouldn't do it for my January.

I'm practically twitching when I get back to the estate. Sleep sure as fuck doesn't come as I hit up Dario for the file he has on January.

I know he's done his research on all May's acquaintances, and I'm not wrong. Smirking, he hands it over, but not without a warning. "It's not a lot, but if you're like me, you're not going to like it. Read up and behave. I'm getting my woman tomorrow night."

"Thanks. I'll be grabbing mine as well."

"Good." An hour later, I've read all they had on her. She's twenty-two and is working as an intern at a news station that broadcasts nationally. She's brilliant, having gotten straight A's in high school and in college.

She went to community college. Her bank account is pretty empty and her credit is basic. Other than one giant student loan, she doesn't have anything on here.

Her parents are listed here, including their finances, which look pretty sweet. They have enough money to pay her tuition, which isn't a lot, but it looks like they cut her off for some reason. I'm not sure why, but they could have helped with community college for sure. Fucking cunts.

Before the internship, she worked at a grocery store since she was sixteen. Damn, the girl is used to hard work and dedication. I stare at the photo I stole from Johnson's apartment and the candid ones the men had gotten from the surveillance.

She's so fucking beautiful. Her long, amber reddish hair is in a messy bun with loose stands being blown by the wind in two pictures. I want to wrap it up in my fist and bring her face to mine, dragging her lips close so I can kiss them and taste their pillowy softness.

The more I stare at the photos, the more jealous I get. It's a little too fucking much and that pisses me off. Why? I don't know. It's not like it's truly personal, but it's not their right to have my woman's information. Still, it gives me what I need to make it through the next twenty-four hours.

CHAPTER TWO

JANUARY

THE ALARM ON MY PHONE GOES OFF WAY EARLIER than I'd like for the trip I dread. Shutting it off, I see a message from Jason.

Problems at home. Need to have a late start. Meet me at the station by six.

Something's weird. He never lets his family life get in the way, like ever. The man didn't mention his family, and he stayed late every single day.

I switch my alarm time and give myself another hour of sleep. Unfortunately, sleep doesn't come. A certain person pops into my head—a brutish-looking stranger.

As I was coming home from work yesterday, there were two men getting into a vehicle; one of them had exited our apartment building, but it wasn't him who caught my attention. His buddy that stood by the vehicle drew my notice. I stayed out of view, but I couldn't hide the way my body shivered from his brutish appearance.

Six foot seven, and a wide frame full of muscles packed in a well-tailored suit. My mouth salivated as he pushed off the vehicle, lowered his sunglasses, peering around to check out the area. My heart danced in my chest while my stomach flipped. Those hawklike eyes stared with intent, and I wanted to know what he'd think if he saw me.

As it was, he didn't notice me in my usual hiding spot that I use when Randall—the sicko—Johnson comes creeping out of his apartment, waiting for one of us girls to appear. This man can bump into me, stalk me all he wants, although I bet he didn't even know I existed.

I stared at his facial hair and wondered what it would feel like to touch it. Then again, he looked like the kind of guy who didn't let strangers get close to him. Hell, I bet people he knew didn't get too close, either. My eyes moved to his hands which were massive just like the rest of him, or well a girl could imagine.

He wasn't wearing any jewelry except for a watch, but from that distance I couldn't make out the type of timepiece. He had an air about him that sent a dangerous chill through me. Even in a suit, I could feel the darkness in him and for some reason, I wanted to explore it.

Would he come back here? What if he stops by here this afternoon like the day before and I'm not here? Why do I care?

By the time I run through all the reasons and a dozen other questions, my alarm goes off again. "Damn it. It's time to get ready," I mutter, tossing off the sheet. Once I'm done getting dressed, I gather my things to take the train to the station. With everything ready, I get my coffee and in walks May, shocked.

"Hey, girl. What's up?" she asks, looking at me with questions.

"Change of plans. He asked me to delay our trip by two hours."

"Oh, okay. Well, be safe, and remember—if he tries anything, use the knife."

"I will, without a doubt." We give each other a hug, and then I head out of the apartment door with my suitcase, my laptop bag, and my purse. When I go downstairs, I try to be quiet so I don't wake up the resident pervert. Hell, I even lift up my suitcase so the wheels don't make a sound as they hit the old ceramic tiles.

A weird smell comes from his doorway, but I can't figure it out. I think it's metallic, but I know he's up to no good. I call the non-emergency line. "There was an odd metallic smell and foul odor coming from my landlord's apartment as I was leaving the building." They ask me several questions, taking my address before I disconnect.

Quickly, I get to the station and then on the train. Once I'm sitting and it takes off, I take a deep breath. I'm running late, so now maybe he'll tell me to forget it and stay here. I doubt it, but a girl can hope. By the time I get to the station, I'm thirty minutes late.

"You made it in, Jan," the station producer says.

My eyes dart around, looking for my jerk boss. "Yes. Where's Jason? Is he flipping his lid?"

"No, he's not here yet."

My brows knit together because there's no way in hell I managed to beat him here. I sure as hell expected to walk in and get canned on the spot. Hell, I almost hoped for it even though it would have put me in a hell of a predicament both financially and professionally. "I'm surprised."

She bites down on her bottom lip, nervously rubbing her thumbnail into her nail beds. "Yes, I expected him to be here already. I have the car he requested and everything."

"He messaged me this morning that he was running late, so I slept in and then there was a delay at the train station."

"Understandable."

She squeezes my forearm lightly. "Get a coffee and a donut. Relax until he gets here." I think she's more nervous than I am about this trip, which makes me wonder if I'm not the first intern he's taken on a field assignment and things didn't quite go as they were supposed to go.

"Thanks." As I take my first bite of a chocolate donut, in walks Jason, looking unfazed by whatever the delay was. In fact, he looks calm and refreshed, as if he's about to give a report on air, stunning both of us who know that's not the man we're used to dealing with. He's a full-blown Divo, and if anything goes wrong, we all know about it.

He gives us a killer smile as he walks up to my side. "Good morning. Sorry for the delay. Finish your donut, and I'll load your luggage. We need to head out. We have a long drive."

"Okay." When his back is turned, both the producer and I share a look of surprise before I finish my donut and rinse it down with another swig of coffee. I use the restroom and meet Jason in the lobby.

"You ready?" he asks, rubbing his hands together. Again, his cheerfulness is over the edge.

Maybe his wife was busy giving him some booty or some head before he left. That would explain why he's so cheery. "Yes."

"Good. Let's go. I have a feeling we'll get everything we need in the next few days," Jason says.

"Fantastic. How long is the drive?" This part is going to be rough.

"It's about twelve hours with gas stops." I nod and then follow him out. He doesn't hold the door open for me, which is good. It would be a change in his personality that would be too much for me to handle. Civility isn't his thing since he thinks he's a king and everyone should cater to him. Hell, I thought he'd make me hold the door open for him.

The first few hours of the trip are good. We make decent time and I almost fall asleep, but I don't want to let my guard down. It could be his plan, so I stay awake by reading up on the target of this exposé we are working on.

My eyes grew heavy about twenty minutes into the dry report, so I cut it short.

Needing to change tactics, I pop in my earbuds and turn on some music while I read on my tablet. It's already one and we were forced to stop for gas around eleven, but now it's time to get some food.

"So was that book any good?" he asks. I knew he was spying over my shoulder, but I couldn't tell how much he could read given he had to focus on the road ahead.

"It was decent. I could drive if you'd like," I offer, wanting to take some control of the situation and maybe learn a little more about where we were going. He kept a lot of it to himself, explaining that as a reporter, he held a lot close to the vest because of stories leaking.

"Not going to happen. I like my life, and you're not old enough to drive a rental without the added insurance."

"Are you serious?" I ask, losing my temper a bit more than I should.

"Yes." I roll my eyes at the bullshit. I'm twenty-two and more than qualified to drive, although I can't say the last time I was behind the wheel. Shit, it's been four years or so, about when I stopped speaking to my parents completely.

They cut me out of their lives the day I turned eighteen. It was like I didn't matter anymore. Since then, I've decided that I'd never trusted people's kindness before I learned their motives again.

We get back on the road, and I shoot May a message before she worries too much.

Almost there. He's been on his best behavior, surprisingly. Miss you.

Within twenty seconds, I get a reply: *Good. I miss you too. Shank if need be.*

I close the message so Jason can't see it, and then I start scrolling the news.

Man killed in Northside Chicago apartment. Possible other illicit criminal activity motive.

As I continue to read the article, I hold in my shock and try to relax. I already know who killed our landlord, but why didn't May tell me about it when I messaged her? It's obvious that it made the news, so she has to be aware of it.

Is she involved with those guys? The man at the diner she mentioned... could he have seen him hitting on May and lost it? No...that's crazy because the guy outside my apartment had to be the killer.

Hell, I knew that handsome goon had hitman written all over him. Those broad shoulders, thick arms, large chest, chiseled jaw, dark eyes, stern presence; he had it all. They think it was a trafficking or prostitution issue? Pictures of women were found in the apartment. I'm not sure why he was killed, but my gut tells me it was the guy standing outside the apartment.

"What's got you so tense? Huh?" my perverted boss asks, reaching out to touch my thigh while he drives.

He's been too fucking nice to me since this morning. I know he's only trying to seduce me while we have time alone.

I quickly shove his hand off my leg. "My landlord was killed last night."

"What? And you didn't know before you left?" he asks, mouth dropping open.

"No, of course not. They found his body today, so I read the article online just right now." He pulls off to the side of the road. "What are you doing?"

"Let me see it." He snatches my phone without my permission and begins to read the article. I'm glad I closed May's text messages where she reminded me to shank him if he gets out of control because he seems to be slipping now.

He actually appears to have paled. I tilt my head and ask him, "Are you okay?"

"Um…yes." He tosses my phone back at me, and then he takes out his phone and sends a message to someone and then gets one right back. It's nuts, but then he starts driving again.

I look at him and see his knuckles are white and flexed tightly against the leather. "Are you sure?"

"I said I am," he shouts. "Just sit back and relax." I do, and he pulls back onto the highway. We still have a little while before we arrive at the cabin in the Ozarks. Shit, I think I'm in the car with not just a pervert, but also a fucking monster. Perhaps I should have kept that to myself, although I'm not sure why my landlord's death should affect him.

I'm quiet and nervous. If I was on edge around him before, it's only amplified with his psycho behavior. He's gone from one extreme to the next in a matter of minutes.

"We have two more hours until we reach our cabin. I don't need you sulking all the way there. Start researching the story we're working on. I want all the details on the political scandal before anyone else." He suddenly turns into more like a patronizing boss again.

Mentally, I'm cursing him out with every word I have in my arsenal while giving him a polite smile. After all, I'm a young intern, intent on growing my career and I don't want to blow it, or so I want him to believe.

"Yes, of course." It's not like I wasn't already doing that earlier, but I will continue if it keeps him off my ass. The sickly sweet Jason is a much better person than this weirdo. Although, I'm not sure why we're looking into issues in Missouri. I know we're a national station, but you'd think it would be something reporters from the region would be on.

I pull out a pad of paper and jot down notes, but since he's looking over my shoulder every once in a while, I can't just text May that I need help. Suddenly, the internet cuts out. Shitballs. This isn't good.

"It looks like it's spotty. We must be getting close."

"With all the surrounding wilderness, I don't doubt it." Then it sinks in. He's had me conducting research for the sole purpose of keeping me preoccupied and unaware of the route we are taking and any specific landmarks. Panic shoots down my spine, but I remind myself that this is just another challenge that I can handle easily.

May's call starts to come in, but then goes out before I can answer it. "Shoot. She's probably checking up on me." It sucks that I can't get calls, but I have some internet signals coming through here and there. Even then, it's been slow and I've had to refresh the page several times.

"You're safe with me." I'm totally not safe at all.

"She's my best friend and, well, that's what besties do. Besides, accidents happen."

"So true," he says, sounding a little too damn ominous for my liking.

"Maybe when we stop, I'll get a better signal," I say, hoping that it clears up soon because I need to call May. I can't believe this is happening, but I do have my knife if necessary. Still, he seems like it might not work.

"More than likely. So what were you able to dig up?"

"Well, he's here this weekend, as well as the congresswoman from Denver." We start going into a normal work conversation that almost calms me down, but I haven't forgotten the violent mood he's been in.

"Perfect."

"Exactly." This scandal would be pretty good if I was getting it on my own and not having to worry about Captain Crazy next to me.

"We're getting very close. It shouldn't be too long before we reach the cabin." He appears to know exactly where to go without GPS, and I'm not liking it.

"Have you been to this place before?" I asked. It's too damn suspect.

"Not to this specific one, but I've been to the Ozarks plenty of times since I was a kid." Interesting. A well-placed sense of fear fills the pit of my stomach. He never mentioned that before and now the look on the producer's face makes a lot more sense.

I have to sneak away. It's consuming my thoughts as we make our way to the cabin. The closer we get, the more my heart races. I let down my hair so he can't see the rapid beating of my pulse when he turns my way which I find to be happening every few minutes. The tension in the car builds, but it's not the sexual kind like he's aiming for. No, I'm ready to run because he's scaring me without saying a word.

Finally, we pull up to the cabin, and the sky darkens. Rain begins coming down in sheets when it was just fucking dry as a bone and sunny as hell a little while ago. Shit, could it be any creepier? A knife might not be enough, and I can't just attack him for no reason. What if he doesn't even do anything and I'm just imagining he's nuts?

We unload the suitcases, and all the while, he's on edge. The cabin is small, a little too small for the two of us, and definitely too low class for the likes of my boss. It doesn't make sense how he'd accept staying here instead of a

Hilton or something like that. I don't say anything because he gets on his phone immediately, pacing around the main room.

He's been on the phone for the past five minutes with someone named Nick, and it doesn't sound good. He's hush-hush around me, but I can see that he's anxious about whatever it is.

Something is going on, and it has to do with my landlord. I'm sure of it. There's no question in my mind because he went from his normal douchebag behavior to this erratic, manic paranoid pacing. The wide-eyed staring and the psycho look are starting to really freak me out.

My suitcase is too heavy to leave with, so I'll have to carry just my large purse. Grabbing both of them, I move toward the bedroom.

"What are you doing?" he asks when he turns and sees me leaving the room.

I turned around and put on the best performance of my life. With a scrunched-up face, I bring up the collar of my tee shirt and wipe my neck. "I'm going to take a quick shower. It was a long drive and I feel kind of gross."

He half smiles and then says, "Oh. Don't use all the hot water."

"I'll be fast." I take my things into the bedroom and then lock the door. There's a large window that leads into the woods. Fuck, it's not quite safe, but I do myself a favor and take a screenshot of the Google map of the area. Once

I start running, I'll lose signal. Needing the area around the cabin, I take extra shots just in case I get really lost.

I pack my large purse with some essentials, including another pair of socks and shoes. Then I send my bestie a message just in case something happens to me.

In serious trouble. My boss has lost his mind. Don't call, but I'm sneaking out and running into the woods. If I can't be found, look there.

I tuck my phone away and then turn on the shower. While it's running, I open the window and slide out, but I barely get ten feet when a hand comes over my mouth, muffling my scream. "Where are you going?"

CHAPTER THREE

ENRICO

AFTER WE DEALT WITH JOHNSON, I STEWED IN rage all night, unable to sleep. All thoughts were on January. I searched her information, gathered everything from the files the men had put together, and read every drop of ink printed up on my woman. The more I learned the more I wanted to know. I don't think it will ever be enough, but I wonder what she'll think of me.

She was perfect for me. Fierce, smart, beautiful, and determined. In fact, she was too damn good for me, but that didn't mean I could fight the emotion that punched me in the chest when I saw her, or stared at her photo.

I'd have to make her see that she was mine and that we would be perfect together. After all, her friends were going to be married to my friends, so it should be a little easier to do the persuading.

Unable to stay in place, I have to speak with Dario and explain to him what's happening. He and Alessio are already in his office. "Dario, Alessio, I am acquiring January for questioning today."

"Good. She's a reporter, and she's been looking into matters more than we already believed. Luca put a recording device in their apartment the other day and recorded her conversation with May. It was very telling." There's a smile on my boss's face. "She plans on listening in on Coleman when she returns, which will not be possible."

He's smiling with that revelation, but I'm not. "When she returns?" My eyebrows shoot up and tension rolls through my body.

"Yes. She's going on a trip with her boss." Instantly, I'm itching to run the fuck out of his office and hunt her down.

"What the hell do you mean she's away with her boss?" I roar.

"Yes, he…"

"He?" I don't realize I've pulled my blade out my sheath, ready to stab this boss who is nowhere near me.

"Calm down. You're supposed to be questioning her about Coleman and the landlord. Is there more?" Alessio asks.

Raging violence sends my mind into overdrive. "He's got a death wish that I'll gladly grant," I say through clenched teeth.

"Another one bites the dust," Alessio says, smirking in amusement. I'm sure they're both getting a kick out of my newfound change, but nothing is funny to me at the moment.

"I don't know. They're in the Ozarks in a cabin doing some reporting, or so that's what I'm told." Dario hands over the information.

"The fuck they are." I shake my head because there's no way they're all the way over there to do reporting. Why are they in a cabin unless they're talking about deforestation or some shit?

"They have a head start on you. According to the audio, they left this morning. They should be there in a few hours," Dario adds.

"I need to stop him and protect her," I muttered, pacing back and forth as I consider my options.

"You need to be careful. He's a national reporter, and too many dead bodies around the girls will be obvious." I hear his warning loud and clear.

"Understood. I need to get there before they do. If he gets her into a cabin alone, anything can happen."

"You're right. So take the plane, load a Rover, and have Vito fly you to the closest landing strip and drive the rest of the way. I'm sure you'll make it before they do," Alessio says.

"See, that's why he's my second," Dario adds, giving him a wink.

"And here I thought you were losing your edge," I say to Alessio.

"I won't let another man get a hold of my woman. She gives you shit, tie her up and toss her in the trunk," he adds.

I make a mental note of that because from what I read, that might actually happen. "Another good one."

"I hate to say this again, Enrico, but don't kill the reporter yet. I know it's not fair and you're going to want his head, but we have witnesses knowing she left with him, and if she appears with you, we'll be implicated immediately. He's a nationwide sensation."

"Understood, loud and clear. I only want her."

Dario nods, standing as he shoots off a message to someone. He then fixes his suit jacket. "Good. I'll get you anything else you need, but for now, if you'll excuse me, I have to prepare for my queen, and you have to find a way to get the story from your reporter."

I charge out of the room, sliding my knife into the sleeve and head straight to my vehicle. I call Vito next. "We have a mission, and I need you now."

"I just got a text from Dario. He said prepare the plane," he says. Damn, Dario was sending that message as we spoke.

"Yes, we're flying over the Ozarks."

"Oh, so you need a drop?" he questioned.

"Yes, but I'll need a ride back."

"Okay. I'll load the vehicle, too. I can land at a secure location, and you can drive the rest of the way there." That's the plan Alessio suggested, but I'm fucking antsy as fuck and want to get to her as soon as possible.

"It would be faster to fly me over and drop me off at her location and then meet me with the vehicle."

"It would be, but that's more dangerous," Vito reminds me.

"I don't give two fucks. He's alone with my woman in a cabin in the woods," I snarl on the phone as I speed home.

"Okay. I'll be ready."

"Sounds good to me. Meet me in twenty minutes. I'm loading what I need." He ends the call and I get myself together fast. I meet him at the hangar, greeting him with a tip of my chin.

He rubs his hands together. "Let's do this." He's always down for some fun, without question. As long as it involves flying, Vito is game.

We arrive at the airport and load the plane. There's just one problem. I need exact coordinates, just in case he moves them from the cabin listed in their itinerary that was given to the station. I call Dario, who suddenly seems irritated. "I can't talk right now. Call Flavio. He'll have everything you need. Tell him I said it's priority number one."

"Thanks."

I call him next. "Hey, Enrico. What's up, man?"

"I need you to give me the location for a phone."

"Sure. This is all simple shit, you know, right?" he says, getting bold as fuck when I'm in a dangerous mood. He's fucking lucky that he's not in front of me and I need this information right now.

"Whatever. I'm about to go hunting, Flavio."

"Sorry, yes." I could picture him throwing his hands up in surrender as he apologizes. When I go hunting, that means I'm ready to end everyone in my path. Don't piss me off. Flavio knows what it's like to be on the wrong side of my blade, only to be saved by Dario who could use his help. Since then, he understands that I'm not the kind of person to piss off.

"Do you just want location, or do you want call logs and text messages?" he asks. I'm glad he can do more than just track it.

"Can I get them in real time?" I hope the fuck so.

"I can clone it so you get everything as it happens."

A face-splitting grin spreads over me. "That's great."

"Here you go. It's sent to your phone. Do you need anything else?"

"Actually, can you track another number? I just need to keep tabs on location."

"Sure." I give him the information, and he sends me the tracking information. "You need anything else?"

"No, I'm good, but you need a woman to toughen you up, Flavio," I say with a chuckle. "Thanks. It's a lifesaver."

"Anything you need." I hear him chuckle.

I hang up and then check the message, allowing me to access her phone. They're together, but then the tracking is spotty. The terrain and signal could make it difficult to track them.

Vito takes off from the private hangar, and we're in flight for over an hour. I'm growing more and more anxious, checking the damn tracker, but it doesn't do me any good at this point because they aren't close to their destination yet.

The messages between January and May calms me down a bit. It's good to know that he hasn't tried anything, and it's clear she's not interested in him. I want to know more about her, damn it.

Unfortunately, I can't read her previous messages like a sick stalker, but I resign myself to the fact that in a few hours I'll see her beautiful face and ask her all the questions I need answering.

"How about I drop you off at a private landing strip? You can take the vehicle and park in the trees. You never know if you'll need it," Vito says as we get closer to Missouri.

"It's probably for the best, even though it might take an hour longer." The way I drive, it will take half that time, but I don't want her running through the woods or trying to get away from me. It's not like she's aware of her future.

As we land at a private landing strip, I check the tracker and find the fucker jumped course. It looks like he's taking her to a secluded cabin farther off the beaten path than the one they were scheduled to be at.

The satellite capabilities of the map show me a small cottage that looks like it hasn't been well taken care of and probably not their actual location. Shit, I need to get there fast before they get there. It's still a far distance from both of us, but they'll reach it first.

It's starting to get dark when I finally arrive. I scope around the entire cabin with my listening device, trying to locate the two, praying I don't catch that fucker with my woman in a compromising position. He's on the phone to someone named Nick, and he's snarling about Johnson's death. It couldn't be, could it?

We were already tracking his phone; that's why it was so easy to find him. The phone goes off in my pocket, and I can see that she's taken screenshots of Google Maps. Then it's a new message to May. Fuck. This one isn't fun or happy.

I'm around the corner just in time to see her jump out the window. The fucking woods are dangerous, especially for someone like her without any experience as the sun goes down.

I quickly wrap her up in my arms with my hand around her mouth. "Where are you going?"

She kicks me in the balls, sending me to my knees, and takes off running into the woods. "Fuck."

Unable to wait for the pain to subside, I hobbled in her direction out of sight of the window and into the tree line. I can hear her feet crunch the wet and mucky leaves throughout the wilderness.

Then she gets as quiet as she can, but the rain has stopped, not doing her any favors.

Damn. I listen for the next noise, not hearing anything until she moves again. I'm two feet away, but she's too slow and I have her. When I nab her, I'm not letting her get the best of me and I'm quick to throw her over my shoulder, snatching her bag away from her.

I carry my scared and brave woman to the waiting Rover and slide her into the back seat, tying her hands and feet before strapping her into her seat belt.

She attempts to spit at me, but I move too fast, reading her much better now. "You animal. I knew you were evil. Why are you doing this? I didn't see anything. I swear I wasn't going to tell anyone that I saw you there at the apartment. Fuck, I don't care that my piece-of-shit landlord is dead." Shit, she saw us?

"Sweetheart, I don't give a fuck about that. I came to get you away from that boss of yours. Now—calm down and maybe if you behave, I'll untie you, but until you do, I'm afraid you can't be trusted, my fiery beauty."

"I'm not your anything," she hisses. I'd take that to heart if she didn't stare at me with a hint of desire behind that fear.

"We'll see." I brush my lips against her forehead and then close the door. I get in the front seat and start the engine, driving through the woods.

"You're a sick asshole. I don't believe you." She sits back, though, quietly looking out the window.

"You can believe whatever you want, but I got the message you sent to May."

"Yeah, because you're probably stalking us, right? Or is your friend interested in my friend?" I can't say she's wrong about either of those things. In fact, she's one hundred percent correct.

"Spot on, but that's neither here nor there."

"So where are you taking me?"

"Back to Chicago." We're so damn far, and I didn't plan ahead. Vito's waiting at the airport for me, though.

"You came all the way over here just to get me away from my boss?" Yes, but not because I give a fuck about any story. I worry that he's going to put his hands on what's mine, and the bastard in me just won't allow it.

"Yes. You know more than you should, and it's my job to figure out what that is. I need to know everything about you, January," I explain.

There's a call on my phone, but it's actually January's, which rings at the same time. "You're a piece of work."

"It's your boss."

"What are you going to tell him?" she asks as if I give a fuck about answering to the likes of him. If I had my way, he'd be hanging upside down in the cabin by his balls.

"I'm not answering it. I don't give a fuck. You're the one who fucking jumped out of the window to escape the fucking prick. He's lucky I don't head back there and snap his fucking neck."

"Why would you do that?" she asks. I can't tell her the real answer just yet.

"Why would you feel the need to jump out the window into the woods?" I toss out.

"I asked you first."

"Because you felt the need to run from him. You were frightened."

"I'm frightened of you. You're going to kill yourself too?"

I crack up in laughter, which causes her tiny nostrils to flare. "Bullshit, princess. You are far from frightened of me. You'd shut your pretty mouth, or you'd be playing nice instead of trying to piss me off. Now, relax and be a good girl."

"I'll never be a good girl for you." She narrows her eyes at me, glaring with an evil promise to give me trouble. I don't mind.

"Then I suppose you enjoy being tied up," I offer, loving the fiery temper she has. It's sure as fuck better than the frightened little woman who jumped out a window to escape a fucking predator.

"I suppose you enjoy kidnapping and tying up women." Interesting...is she jealous?

"It's a first. Nice change."

My phone rings another ten times, and it's all her boss trying to find her. We're on the road toward the airport landing strip when I see the damn rental car. "He's fucking behind us."

Shit. It's then that Flavio calls me, and I put him on speaker. "What's up?"

"Hey, Enrico, sir. I just wanted to let you know that other number you gave me... Well, it's tracking the first number. They aren't together and, well, it's calling it, and now it's just left the location and following it."

"Son of a bitch. This bastard wants to play with me." Dario's words come back in my head, reminding me that I have to remain in control and not filet the creep.

"Sorry, sir. I thought you wanted to know."

"No, it's good, Flavio. You did good. I owe you a gift. I'll call you back in a minute. It's time to deal with my problem."

I answer the phone when it rings again. "Hello, Mr. Sizemore. Is it protocol for you to stalk your assistant?"

"What the fuck do you mean? Who are you, and why have you kidnapped my assistant?"

"I haven't kidnapped her. I rescued her when she jumped out of her window, which you knew damn well. Why are you tracking her?"

"She's more than my assistant. She's my fiancée."

"Bullshit, fuckface. You're married, so beat it before I handle you."

He's still following me. "What's that supposed to mean?" I finish the call without giving him a response, and then I turn off her phone as well as the cloning link to lose the tracking, so I call Flavio and move into the main traffic away from the airport.

"Can we hack it and have him track someone else's phone?"

"Sure."

"Okay. Do that. Send him on a wild goose chase."

"Yes, sir. I'll be tracking it. Do you need anything else?"

"No. I'm good." I ended the call.

"He's tracking me?" she gasps. I can see her shaking. Fuck. There's a car that I recognize nearby and it's his, but then suddenly it's turning off toward another direction. Good.

"Hold on." I pull into a nearby hotel parking lot. I call Vito. "Take the plane back. I'm going to drive."

"Okay. Are you sure you're good?"

"Yes."

"Let me know if you need anything. I'll let the boss know."

"Thanks." I hang up and check my surroundings several times before I open the door and slide into the backseat. Pulling her into my arms, I hold her tightly. "Calm down, January. I'm not going to let him hurt you, ever."

"He was going to find me. What does he want with me?"

"I don't know." I have a feeling, but we don't need to discuss that. I have to get her inside a hotel and in a warm bath with some food so she can get regulated and back to a rational state of mind. Her shaking is scaring me. I never want her to hurt in any way, shape, or form.

I keep her tied up and check into the hotel only to find her pressing on the damn horn. "Fucking shit." I whip open the door and snap off on her. "Do you want him to come back and find your ass?"

"No." I nudge her ass back in her seat and pull into the spot outside our door and park.

She's so small compared to me that I toss her over my shoulder and swat her ass. "Behave or I'll make things worse for you, little girl." Luckily all the entrances are from the outside and we're on the first floor. I unload her with my emergency blanket over her so it looks like we're avoiding the rain as I carry her into the room.

Once inside, she tries to throw herself out of my arms, but she's still tied up so I toss her pretty ass on the bed.

"Sweetheart, why must you give me a hard time? I'm trying to help you." I groan and stare at her in frustration. She's beautiful, even with her face flushed, hair messy and tied up. In fact, maybe I find her even sexier. I need to get a hold of that tension.

"You've kept me tied up," she reminds me.

"You kicked me in the balls after I tried to save you from going straight into danger."

"I didn't know who had me."

"You knew damn well it wasn't that asshole." She looks right at me, knowing the truth.

"Then you fucking tried to draw attention to yourself instead of behaving while I was trying to keep you from going into complete shock."

"I'm sorry about that. It was stupid." She bows her head shamefully.

I slide my finger under her chin, tipping her head upward to meet my eyes. "I'm going to untie your pretty little ass and then feed you, okay?"

She nods. I undo her ankles and then her hands. "Here you go." I expect her to suddenly fight me, but she doesn't. Instead, she rubs her wrists, which makes me feel like a big old heel. I sit at the foot of the bed and take off her shoes and socks. Once her tiny feet are bare, I grab them and set them on my lap, massaging her poor feet.

"Don't; they must be gross." She reaches down, trying to stop me.

I wrap her wrists in one of my hands and stop her. "I don't give a fuck. I feel like a prick for having hurt you at all.

Now, relax and let me make it better. What do you want to eat? I'm sure you're hungry."

"Do you think we can get any food here?" I hear her belly rumble and she presses her hands to it, blushing immediately.

I check the menus that are on the nightstand table. "There are a few restaurants right around the corner."

"It's storming out there."

"According to the radar, it's going to lighten up. Besides, they will deliver for the right price. Now what do you want, princess?" I toss them on the bed next to her and then walk over to the window, checking for that asshole. My tracker shows him out, around twenty minutes from us. That's good news because he's far away from her and I can keep my word to Dario.

"I'm not a princess. I've never been a princess," she says in a whisper, but I hear the sadness in her voice.

I turn around and kneel down in front of her. "You should be a princess."

"What do you want from me? I don't have any special information, and I don't plan on going to the cops about seeing you in front of the apartment."

"I told you I don't care about that."

"Then what's your motive? Because you didn't just come after me because my boss was a pervert."

"I did."

"But the message wasn't sent until right now."

"I didn't say it was because of the message. The thought of you being alone with him at all was enough for me. Princess, I'll explain this to you right now. From the moment I saw your photo, I wanted you like a madman. There's no other motive."

"So you want to fuck me. Then what?"

"Then I want to do it again and again until you're carrying our babies." She doesn't respond, but she presses her lips together several times and then opens her mouth, unable to speak. I've clearly startled my future wife, but I get the feeling she isn't revolted.

"Enough of that talk. Let's get some food."

"Okay."

"May I use the bathroom?" she asks me, scooting to the edge of the bed.

"There's no other exit out that way."

"I'm not trying to get away. I just haven't peed in hours, if you must know."

"Sure. Let me help you."

"I don't need you to help me pee."

"Fine. Go ahead." She stands up, and I can't keep my eyes off her ass. When she finally closes the door to the bathroom, I call the guys, wanting more information on this fucking reporter who had my woman at his mercy.

I get a hold of Alessio, who asks for details. "He was tracking her movements," I snarl.

"Are you sure?" he asks.

"Yes, Flavio told me that he was on our tail, and we were able to thwart him."

"Fuck. Well, it's good that you went after her when you did."

"Where's Dario?"

"He's dealing with Coleman at the moment." I get it. The bastard is going to meet his end. Fuck, I wish I could be a part of that situation.

"I should be back tomorrow or the day after. I need to speak to him as soon as possible."

"I'll tell him to call you as soon as possible." I want a hand in every ass whooping and death that comes from this mess with January and the girls. Every single one of these people are garbage and need to be dealt with.

The bathroom door opens and then January appears. "I've got to go." I quickly hang up and then turn to face her.

"So what's up with my friends?" she asks.

"Nothing that I'm aware of," I lie. There isn't much that I can tell her, so it's best if I say nothing at all. It's not like she can talk to them at the moment anyway. They're both preoccupied or even just sleeping.

"I want to call May. She's probably worried about me."

"Your message never made it to her."

"What do you mean?"

"Your message never went through. The crappy cell range." It's the truth, but from the look on her face she doesn't believe a word of it.

"Oh. Are you saying that, or is there another reason?"

I gesture with my head and answer as politely as I can without saying too much. "No, but I'd wait to call her. She's busy at the moment."

"Are you saying…"

"I don't know what they're doing, but I was told they were busy when I called, so relax. I promise you'll talk to her. Dario knows where I am, and if your message does go through, you'll know because she'll either call you or he will call me. Now, calm down and sit so you can tell me what you want to fucking eat."

"Fine." She stomps over to the bed with a huff.

I didn't mean to come off as a dick, but I don't like lying to her, and yet, I can't tell her what Dario has planned for May.

CHAPTER FOUR

JANUARY

IT TAKES ABOUT FIVE MINUTES OF LOOKING AT the menus for me to pick an all-night burger place that delivers for the right money. I'm not hungry really, but the big brute in the corner of the room, staring me down, refuses to budge on the subject, so I select a place and some food.

"So tell me about yourself, Enrico," I say, hoping to ease the tension running through me. I'm not sure it's possible when someone so sexy is feet away, staring at you like he'd rather eat you than any other meal, but I'm going to try.

He sits down next to me, which only makes things worse because my pulse ramps up and my body turns to Jello.

"What do you want to know? Let me guess. As a reporter —everything?" He smirks, and I see a slight scar on his jawline that makes me curious.

A part of me wants to run my fingers along it and wonder if he'd tell me how he got it. Was it a fight with another mobster? An angry lover scorned? Why does the latter make me jealous?

Shaking off my own irritation, I try to mess with him. "Well, I'm not a full-blown reporter yet, but yes. I don't even know your last name, and it's not like you introduced yourself. I heard your name from that guy on the phone."

He forms an O with his mouth and then nods. "Sorry about that, sweetheart. I should have done that when we first met, but since someone had their foot in my balls, it was a little difficult. My name is Enrico Vincenzo Gennaro Barone."

"Wow, seriously. We're still on that sore subject?" I tease. I'm sure that shot to the balls had to hurt, but in my defense, it felt necessary at the time. "So you have all those names?"

"Yes."

"Or are those just your aliases?" I raise my eyebrow and twist my lips, challenging him.

He just smirks at me, tapping my chin. "Don't need aliases if you've never been caught, sweetheart."

I try to hide the instant raise in my core body temperature and elevated heart rate when he called me sweetheart, so I throw out another challenge. "So you're just really good at kidnapping women."

"I already told you, love. You're the only one, so don't get so jealous." I hate that he's reading me too well which is expected for a man like him.

"Chill that oversized ego of yours. I'm not jealous; I'm gauging my captor."

"I'm not your captor." I cock my brow at him, and then he shrugs. "Well, I suppose I am, but not in a bad way."

"Whatever. So tell me more about you, Enrico Vincenzo Gennaro Barone."

"That smart mouth of yours needs to be punished." Damn, why does that sound like a welcome invitation?

"Yeah, well. I'm here with you, aren't I?" I tease, egging the brute on. There's just something about this strong, intimidating, handsome persona that draws me to him.

"Damn it, girl." He shakes his head, and then there's a knock on the door.

"That better be our food. Don't act up. It won't be good for the delivery person, and I'm sure they have a family to go home to."

"You are an asshole."

"Yes, I am, and I'll do whatever I have to do to keep you safe."

"I'll behave for now so some random stranger doesn't get hurt." He goes to the door, and I don't see who the person is but I hear the woman's voice, and instantly I don't like her. It's husky and sensual, like she has plenty of experience with men like Enrico. I grumble as she chats with him about his needs.

"He doesn't need anything else," I hissed, stepping up beside him. "He didn't order a hooker with his meal. If he wanted stale fish, he would have ordered it. Now be gone." I nudge my way between the door and him and slam it shut with a bit too much attitude. "Are we going to eat, or are you going to let my food get cold while you chase tail?"

"Sweetheart, the only pussy I crave is too fucking feisty to get a hold of. You need to eat before you bite my dick off."

"You wish I got that close to your dick."

"You will, and you know it. Don't fucking deny you want me. Or keep denying it, and you'll be longing to ride this cock sooner or later." I roll my eyes and snatch the bag of food because he's not wrong.

"Keep dreaming."

"It's sure as hell going to be a hot dream tonight," he says, leaning in and brushing his lips against my hair.

"Just eat."

He gives me that curled up smile before licking his lips and staring right between my legs. "I thought you'd never…"

"I meant the takeout," I glare, doing my best to keep my body from reacting.

"Hand it over." He reaches out, snatching the bag from me this time and smiling, moving over to the small table and chair that look like they've seen better days and taking a seat.

When he notices that I haven't taken my eyes off him, he gives me a wink. I flip him off and sit on the bed to eat my food because it's too dangerous to sit next to him. Why am I letting him get to me?

We don't say anything as we eat our food, and the silence is uncomfortable. Not since my freshman year in high school was I nervous eating in front of people, and that was in front of the cool girls, but this is different.

Enrico's eyes continue to lift up from his food, focusing on me, but it's not to keep an eye on me. It's something else entirely. There's a wicked gleam in his eyes that should scare my virginal self, but it doesn't. No, I long for it, want to see what he'd do to me if he let loose the brute inside.

"Are you enjoying your meal?" I ask.

"Yes, but I could be having a better meal." He wags his brows up and down, staring right at the apex of my thighs again.

"Sorry, you're on guard duty tonight. You can go look for a woman tomorrow after you drop me off."

"Not going to happen. I already found my woman. Now, finish your food."

"Yes, sir." I salute him and then go back to eating my burger and refuse to look at him again so I don't know if he truly has his eyes on me even though I can feel those intensely devilish ones on me.

We go back to that uncomfortable silence while we munch down on some greasy food that I'm sure will not be good for my figure. He finishes before me, tossing his trash in the can next to him.

"Thank you for the food and the massage," I say, setting my wrappers in the trash.

"You're welcome. Now, it's time to get some sleep." It's the last thing on my mind right now.

"Sleep? Where are we sleeping? There's only one bed," I boldly remind him, which I'm sure he hasn't missed.

"We'll be sharing it. Relax. I'll behave myself. As much as I want you naked, I only want you coming to me of your own free will."

"Fine, I'll kick you in the balls again if you do try anything," I say.

"That's understandable. Just keep them knees and feet to yourself until I deserve it, princess. Come on. I'm tired, and I'm sure you're exhausted." I'm only in my tee shirt and panties when I slide under the covers.

He sets a thing of zip ties on the nightstand as a warning. "I promise I won't run."

He turns off the light and strips out of his outer clothes until he's in just his boxers, but I can still make out the silhouette of his body from the bathroom light. "Good girl. Now go to sleep." I feel the bed move as he maneuvers his large frame next to mine. Why does it feel so good?

It's just plain freaking wrong. He kidnapped me, damn it. Yes, he saved me from my boss and from my own ridiculous plan to run into the wilderness, but he still kidnapped me.

"What are you mumbling about over there?" he growls out.

"Um, nothing. Geez, you kidnap a girl then have complaints about her thoughts while she tries to clear her head."

"Get some sleep. We're heading back to Illinois tomorrow, and it's a long drive."

Wow, someone is getting crabby. "Did you drive all the way here?"

"No, I flew in."

"Then why aren't we flying back?"

"Because we had a fucking tail on us, and I wanted to lose him before he got any personal information and linked it back to my boss."

"Oh, yeah." I nod in the darkness because that's smart.

"Yeah, your boss might be a sick fuck, but he's also a reporter with a lot of connections."

I reach over on my side and turn on the side lamp, sitting up in bed. I ask, "Are you always this grumpy?"

"I have a lot of tension right now," he grumbles, covering his eyes with his strong forearm, displaying his epically awesome muscles. My pulse kicks up a notch, and I ache so much just visualizing his arms around me again.

"Maybe you're the one who needs a massage," I say, reaching out to touch his ripped bicep.

"That's not a good idea," he growls, moving fast as hell and sitting up, so I can't make contact with his muscular arm.

"Why not?" I ask.

"I thought I fucking explained it." I slowly move my head from side to side. "Because I want you on my cock, screaming my name as you take every inch of me while I beat up that pussy. And frankly, massaging me isn't going to stop that from going away."

"You shouldn't say things like that," I answer with a pout, sounding more like a naughty schoolgirl than I mean to be.

Honestly, I'm so turned on; I want to ride his cock, his face, or any part of him he'd let me. It's terrible because he's not the kind of man I should be attracted to, especially since he kidnapped me, but heaven have mercy on me because resisting the urges rushing through me is getting harder and harder as every moment passes.

"Why is that?" he asks, reading me easily.

I stiffen my back and puff up my chest, crossing my arms over my breasts in a huff. "Because it's not polite. We're supposed to be sharing a bed without you fucking me." I have to create the illusion that I don't desire him.

He stares at me and I can feel the tension bloom between us. "Exactly. So keep your tiny hands to yourself and go to sleep."

Maybe I could use those zip ties on him if he falls asleep.

"Little girl, I can break through those zip ties." Shit, he heard me. He quickly wraps them around his wrists, tightening them with his mouth to the point that they are nearly cutting off his circulation, and with a rapid tug, tears them right off. "Do you want to try me?"

"Jackass." He smirks.

I give him a light shove and stick my tongue out at him. He glares and then reaches over me. I freeze, thinking he's going to lean in and kiss me, but instead, he continues past my body, turning off my nightstand light. "Go to bed before I forget my manners and bury my big dick inside your wet pussy or let that tongue of yours lick my cock like a damn lollipop."

I slide back down under the covers and the turn to give him my back. There's no way I want him to see my flushed face or my soaked panties.

I can't speak because I might confess that I want him inside my drenched, untouched hole. The man has a filthy mouth, and he wants to dirty up my mouth too. Damn it, I'm tempted to let him.

Closing my eyes, I try to rest, but it takes forever for sleep to come.

WHEN I WAKE UP, MORNING LIGHT BEAMS through the windows and I find myself wrapped around the big brute. At first I'm confused, but then I remembered what happened. So I examine the situation ever so slowly. One of my legs is over his hip, my pussy snuggled right against his massive hard-on. Damn, is that thing huge just like the rest of him?

My entire upper body rests on his broad chest while his fingers splay along my ass, his other hand in my hair that's now out of its braid. When did that happen? Not the braid, but our bodies so intertwined. It's like we've been holding each other all our lives and it feels so damn right.

I don't know why I didn't try to run away last night, but I found myself trapped in his embrace, loving his arms around me all night. For the first time in my life, I didn't care what his motives were as long as I was with him. Enrico has a hold on me that is unexplained.

It feels so damn good to have his body under my smaller one. The pull to relieve the ache is too hard to resist, so I rub my wet pussy on his cock, up and down. "I told you about massaging me."

"I'm massaging myself," I answer, grinding on him a little harder. Forgetting everything, but my need and the way this man makes me feel.

"Oh yeah," he whispers. He reaches down between us, sliding my panties to the side and slipping a finger into my wet folds. "You need a massage?"

"Yes," I whimper, feeling his thick finger stretching my untouched hole.

"You're so fucking wet for me this morning." He crooks his finger, pumping in and out of my pussy.

"Enrico. Oh." I press my lips on his chest. He growls and flips me onto my back.

"Woman, you're playing a dangerous game with a dangerous man."

"Would you hurt me?" I ask.

"Never." I believe him, even though I know that's foolish to trust a mobster.

"Then you're not so dangerous."

"I want to fill you up, keep you for the rest of our days, and destroy any man who dares to take you away from me. I'd consider that very dangerous."

Trust is hard for me, but he makes it simple. "I like those motives."

"When it comes to you, my motives are pure."

"Pure?" I challenge him, knowing he's planning to take my purity away. Divest me of the last bit of innocence and it's the one piece I'd gladly give away.

"Purely to make you mine...forever." He crushes his mouth to mine, slipping his tongue inside, delving in and claiming me in a kiss that needs no clarification. My captor's intentions are selfish, and so are mine.

I run my hands through his short, thick hair, eliciting a moan from him. He bites down on my lip, thrusting his finger into my pussy a little more.

"Baby, I'm hungry for breakfast. Are you going to feed me?"

"Do I look like your wife? Feed yourself," I tease, daring him to take control.

"Gladly," he grunts, dragging his face away and down to my chest where he bites through my shirt, nipping my right breast. Unsatisfied with that, he lifts up my top and sucks my nipple into his large mouth, sending my back bowing off the bed.

Wow, I've played with my breasts before and never felt anything like that. His mouth, the heat, his tongue, they send a tingling vibration straight to my core. I cry out, wanting, pleading for more. "More. Brute, give me more."

He slaps my left breast before taking it into his lips, sliding his tongue around my stiffened nipple while he rubs my pussy. I'm about to come undone. "I'm starving, woman."

"Enrico," I whisper as my pussy clenches, aching for his mouth to go south. Sinking lower, his eyes still focus on me, his mouth hovering over my partially covered pussy. With a quick tug, he tears my panties.

"Hey, I liked those."

"Should have served me." He dives into my core, swiping up my juices with his devilish tongue. I grip the sheets in this mediocre room, wondering how in the world I've succumbed to him when I told myself I wouldn't, but there's nothing to be said for it because I know that he's got me right where he wants me, and he's right where I want him too.

"Oh…yes. Please. I'm…yes. That's incredible."

"Tell me, bella mia. I want you coming on my tongue."

"I'm so close." I feel his finger and tongue working to stretch me at the same time, then he sucks on my clit, sending me over the edge. I cry out, coming. "Enrico," I scream his name, thighs shaking, back arching off the bed.

"Take off your top. I want to see your tits. I want to suck on them while I fuck you so damn good, baby." He slides off his boxers as I lift off my top. "That's a good girl." Why does it turn me on when he praises me?

"I've never done this before." He freezes, briefly staring at me, and then he gives me a wicked smile. Damn, the bastard only gets hotter when that dark brooding look switches to a grin.

"That's good, because I'm fucking insane as it is and I'm tempted to go after every ex before me." He pushes the round head through my folds, plunging past my innocence as hands press down on the mattress beside my head. "You're mine, January." Our mouths clash in a needy kiss as I fight off the pain of his cock taking my virginity.

Enrico rocks his body forward, sending his length deeper and then pulling out almost completely before sliding back in. Every time, it's like brand new and I can barely catch my breath at the way he destroys my pussy.

Still, I want more. Clinging to his broad shoulders, I wrap my fingers around them and dig my nails in.

"Fuck, January, baby girl. You're so fucking tight. You're killing me."

"I'm so close, Enrico. Fuck me." He slides his arm around my shoulders and lifts me off the bed so I'm being drilled on his pole while he holds me in his arms. "I'm coming."

"Good girl. Fuck, baby. I'm coming too." He drops his head onto my shoulder, biting down on my skin as he ruts and comes inside of me.

I can't believe we had sex. My hair is a sweaty mess on my forehead and Enrico brushes it aside. "God, you're so beautiful."

His mouth is on mine, kissing me softly. That gentle caress and kiss removed the doubt I had felt a moment earlier. It's too soon to be in love, but our chemistry is insane.

CHAPTER FIVE

ENRICO

"WHAT?" I BARK OUT, NEARLY CRACKING MY phone.

"Yes, my wedding is in about ten minutes, but I spoke to Alessio, and he said the reporter is a crazy stalker for your woman." I want that fucker's head on a spike, but I have a feeling I have to chill.

"The bastard needs to be dealt with," I snarl into the phone in a hushed whisper, hoping that January doesn't hear me.

"In due time, but there's more. I believe he's been working with Coleman, Johnson, and a cop named Nick Thompson." That's fucking four people at least, and all of them are tied to our women. It's not a fucking coincidence.

I'm more than sure it only took one of those assholes to get their hands on the girls before the other avenues were added. They were led into a trap, lured one by one. Fucking hell, we're going to destroy every single one of them.

"I overheard the reporter talking to someone named Nick before I snatched up January," I say.

"Then I'm more than sure he's the asshole reporter helping clean up the disappearances of young women."

Damn it, and I have no doubt he planned to do something with January whether she surrendered to his whims or not. The thought of what could have happened if I hadn't gotten to her in time makes my stomach turn and my anger grow.

"I'm going to kill him. I'm going to find that fucking reporter and end him."

"Hold on, Enrico. We need to handle this carefully. Have Flavio track him down and monitor everything. We'll go from there, and you come back as soon as possible. Until we are secure, we leave that piece of shit alone."

No one should be touching her except me, although right now I think she feels like I shouldn't be touching her either. January's in the bathroom showering my fucking cum off her body, which pisses me off but I can't blame her.

She's still confused about what we are. Soon January will figure out that we're meant to be together because I'm not going to let her go. She'll just have to come to terms with her issues.

"Last we heard, he was tracking someone else, so hopefully he lost our scent and went back to the cabin or to the city."

"Well, contact Flavio and learn more."

"I'll get back to you when I have more information."

"Good. And congratulations."

"Thank you. I hope I can say the same for you."

"I believe you can."

"Good. Congratulations, my friend." I end the call and then feel January standing behind me, but I'm not sure how long she's been standing there. Fuck, I wonder how much of that conversation she heard.

"How was your shower?" I ask, hoping to distract her from any questions her brilliant and inquisitive mind plans on asking.

"It wasn't bad. There's still some hot water. Are you going to take one?" she asks, running her eyes up and down my body. I'm just in my slacks pants and an undershirt.

I need to, but I'm not sure she won't book it out the door. "In a few minutes."

"You don't trust me, do you? You think I'm going to run after what we just shared?" She narrows her eyes at me, and I'm a little ashamed of myself for not giving her the benefit of the doubt.

"Are you planning on running?" I ask, raising my brows and challenging her once more.

She shakes her head and sighs. "No. I don't have anywhere to go."

"Fine. I'll take a shower." I grabbed my belongings while she was in the shower this morning so I wouldn't have to step out again.

Thankfully the area was clear and there was no sign of danger, and according to the text I received from Vito, Jason Strongman never made it to the airfield before he took off, so there was no risk on his end.

Taking my things into the bathroom, I step inside and shower as fast as possible. While I do, I shoot Flavio a message and ask him to call me in ten. Just as I'm getting dressed, he calls. "Hey, I need to track that asshole. Can I do it from the one you sent me last night?"

"Yeah, but I've been keeping tabs on him. I figured you'd want me to do it."

"Good. Tell me what you got." I take the information he gives me and store it for good use, coming up with a plan for later that I'll run past Dario when I return.

There's more to Jason Strongman than I gave him credit for. He's slick and covering his tracks quicker than the wind in a sandstorm. I end the call with him and finally make my way out of the bathroom to find January standing by the window, staring outside.

She turns to me and asks, "Can we stop at my apartment? I need some of my things and as you can see, I need some clothes." I lick my lips because I'd love to see her in nothing but those shorts and that tee shirt, but unfortunately she has a point.

"Yes, we can stop on the way back to the estate."

"Do you live on the estate?" she questioned, raising her brow.

"Yes, I live on one of the properties." Only four of us actually live on the main estate. The rest of the men drive in from their apartments nearby.

"Is the estate huge? How many of you live on it?" she asks in quick succession.

I raise my eyebrows and ask, "Are you doing an investigative report?"

"Of course not. I wouldn't dare." No. I need to be a little more trusting of my woman, but it's hard, all things considered. It wouldn't matter anyway because she's not going to leave my side ever again. I'm going to have her in our home, filled with my cum and thoroughly sated as much as humanly possible, so she'll never want to leave.

A text comes in from Flavio to give him a call. "Give me a moment. I'm going to load the vehicle with our things."

"Okay. I'm going to try May again," she says.

"She's busy," I inform her, but I leave out the whole wedding situation because it's not something she needs to be made aware of just yet. After all, I'm not sure if it's happened or how much I'm allowed to share, or what she'll believe even if I did tell her.

"You keep saying that." She stomps her feet, losing her patience with me, but there isn't much I can do at the moment.

"Yeah, well, she is."

"What are you not saying?"

"Let's just say she's probably getting up to what we were doing this morning."

"Not May. She's not like me. She's a good girl."

"Baby girl, you were a virgin."

"Yes, but she wouldn't give herself to the wrong side of the law."

"People can surprise you."

"They sure do." She sighs again, parking her ass on the bed, rolling her phone in her hands.

"I'll be right back." She nods without looking up at me. When I step outside with our things, I notice a new vehicle nearby. "Flavio, what's up?"

"Hey, the girl called him."

"What girl?"

"The other number you had me track. January Holmes."

"What the fuck?"

"Yes. She called him about twenty minutes ago. I thought maybe you did, but then she sent a text that I knew you wouldn't."

"Oh, hell, no." He forwards it to me, and I'm fucking blown away. She gave him the hotel that we were staying at.

I slam through the doors and grab her around the fucking throat, pinning her to the bed. "Have you lost your fucking mind?"

"What? No. Why are you hurting me?" I let go of her because there's no fucking way I want to hurt her, even though I've never felt so fucking betrayed.

"You called him. You fucking told him where we were. You fucking played me."

"It's not what you think." I grab her again, this time by the biceps to stop her from running away, and then she presses her hands to my arms, rubbing them, gently like she's calming a wild animal.

"Then what is it?"

"Look. I heard you wanted to kill him. I knew he'd say some crazy shit when we got back, maybe make something up about you being involved in my landlord's death. He's a reporter, after all, and they were working together."

"You knew about it."

"I puzzled it out on the drive to the cabin. It's why I had to get away. I got that damn internship way too easily, and now it makes so much sense."

She's too hard on herself. January's smart and intuitive, deserving of being a reporter. I released my hold on her and sit up, pulling her onto my lap.

"Anyway, I called him to say that you were my boyfriend and were pissed off that I didn't tell you about the trip since you were on a covert ops mission in the military."

I chuckled. "What's so funny?" she asks.

"You weren't completely lying."

"You'd just gotten back and flew in to find me. I told him that I knew he was going to seduce me and I wasn't going to let it happen because I didn't cheat."

"So he doesn't think you know anything about your landlord and him?"

"No. I just wanted to make it look like we had a romantic interlude at the hotel here. We didn't go anywhere. That I just wanted to forget about this trip, and we can start over when we get back."

"What did he say?"

"He agreed, as long as you don't beat him up."

I look at her for any markings, but I didn't even leave a red spot on her skin. "I'm sorry."

"You didn't hurt me. I promise."

"But why did you send him an image of your location?"

"I only sent him a picture of a different hotel in the area. It's not the one we're at. It's the one down the road, but it looks like ours." She shows me, and it's not the exact same one. Fuck, now I feel like a bigger asshole.

"Calm down, you big brute. I told you I was fine."

"Are you ready, then?"

"Do we have to leave just yet?" she asks.

"I would like to get a start because the weather isn't looking good. I think we're going to have to spend another night somewhere else."

She smiles, and I lead her out to the truck. Then, I see the people who were in the waiting vehicle, and it's an older couple. I was being paranoid. Just years of experience playing with my head.

We drive all the way back to Illinois, stopping halfway to stay at a nice bed-and-breakfast as another summer storm rolls through. This one is worse than the day before so it's a long night, but this time we make sure to keep ourselves well occupied. January comes louder and harder than the storm while I flood her more than the Mississippi banks.

Finally, we arrived at her apartment building. It's around three in the morning after a long evening of driving. It's good because no one will see us, and we'll be in and out before someone comes looking—like the police.

Yesterday the detective on Johnson's case called, but since she'd been sleeping and had called about the foul odor before she left, they had no other questions for her. They were well aware whoever did this wasn't some small female. Besides, our cleanup crew left just enough evidence to implicate Coleman.

They'll never find him, though.

His body has long since been disposed of, and it looks like he'll be considered a fugitive. His accounts have been emptied and his IDs have been tossed in a shredder in his home office, and his life was quickly packed up, making it clear he fled. Even his vehicle was seen leaving the U.S. into Mexico where it's already been dismantled and parts redistributed, VIN numbers removed and replaced.

Everything is dark in her building, and the street seems deadly silent like it should at this hour. It's a great sign, but I get an uncomfortable feeling, as if there's something lurking in the shadows. If anything, we're here to pick up clothes. After all, she does live here. I can't shake the feeling.

Before we cross to the front door, I clasp her in my arms and kiss her roughly. "What was that for?"

"Just a reminder that I'm not allowing you a chance to run away from me. You're mine and I just can't let you go."

"Oh, okay. I'm not going to run yet anyway. It's too early. The trains don't run twenty-four hours a day," she teases. I swat her ass and then take her hand and lead her up the stairs to the second floor, keeping her body firmly against the wall to protect her.

We make it to her apartment, and the door is slightly ajar. "Hold on."

"Who the hell do you think you are?" a uniformed officer asks, stepping up to us from behind the open door. What the fuck is he doing in her darkened apartment?

"This is my apartment," January says.

"You must be January." How the fuck did he know that off the bat? There are three girls that live here and unless he's already met them today, which he wouldn't since they're at the estate, he's too informed.

"I am…" My girl's onto him as well.

I cut her off and question the bastard. "Where the hell did you come from, Officer, and why the hell are you hiding in the apartment building in the middle of the night?"

"Why are you two slinking in here in the middle of the night?" he questions, flashing his light at us.

"We just arrived back in Chicago, and I came to get some clothes after my trip, but I'm not staying after what happened. Secondly, this is my damn apartment, and I can come and go as I please," she huffs.

"My apologies. You need to be careful because your place was burglarized, Ms. Holmes. That's why I've been asked to watch over the building just in case someone returns." Her mouth falls open and I grow increasingly suspicious.

"Sweetheart, let's get you some clothes and go. We need to get some rest." I grab my phone out of my pocket, but I'm not sure if I should call for backup when I want to shoot this fucker the second I spot his name. Officer Thompson. We step into the apartment and find that it, in fact, has been ransacked.

"What the hell were they looking for?" she sobs. Fuck, it breaks my heart.

I need her thinking straight right now. "Where's your room?"

"That door." I walk her to her room because I don't trust that asshole cop and I'm not sure there isn't trouble waiting inside. I pull out my phone and give Luca a call, whispering the conversation. "Listen, we have a problem at January's apartment. It's been ransacked. There's a cop named Thompson outside. He surprised us in the dark and then questioned us. Don't trust."

"On my way."

"Okay." She stares at the room in dismay, and I want to smash someone's head in. They destroyed her shit, but I can replace it all. She turns to me when a realization hits her.

"Oh my God, wait. That's Thompson," she gasps. I press my hand to her mouth. I'm guessing she heard a lot of my conversation.

"Go get your shit like I told you to—right now," I say in a hushed whisper. We need to move quickly and silently, or we're leaving without her shit.

"Sorry." She steps back as I let her and then grabs a couple of things out of her drawer, but then freezes. "Enrico." I come over, and there's a death threat inside the drawer. *Say a word and die.* It must have been from Thompson but handed down on orders by Strongman. The fucking prick.

"I'll get you new clothes, sweetheart. Let's just go."

She shakes her head. "I need to grab my favorite book."

She moves before I can stop her, and Thompson's waiting. Dust flies in the air, blowing into her face. Shit. I deck the son of a bitch, but as I do, she falls backward onto her ass. I go to help January up, but she's slapping away my hand.

"Get away from me."

She slaps my hands away. "I'm sorry, baby. I didn't mean to knock you down."

"You're a monster. Get away," she shouts. Damn it, I didn't think it was that serious. I'm trying to protect her.

"He is. I'm a cop. I'm here to protect you," the asshole says from his spot on the ground, wiping his busted mouth. I'm about to grab my gun when I think twice about it. Right now, I don't have a story to spin.

"You're a monster too. Oh my God." She panics, eyes glassy as hell. She goes running through the apartment. I'm on her in a second before she heads to the nearest window. Fucking hell, I'm going to kill this bastard for whatever she's on.

A rush of light footsteps can be heard, and I know it's Luca. He comes through the door, finding the cop on the ground. "He blew something in her face."

"Oh my God. Everyone is out to get me," January cries, sobbing into my chest until she realizes I'm holding her again. Then she scratches the shit out of my face.

"Fuck," I growl. Luca tosses me some zip ties from his pocket.

"Here. These won't leave too bad of a mark, but your face might need some treatment. Shit." He looks down at the officer. "Now, what do we have here, Officer Nicholas Thompson? Is this..." He takes a taste of the residue in the vial that the officer has in his pocket. "Um...ketamine?"

"Fuck. She's tripping right now."

"Yes, and since she's scared, this isn't helping."

"Yeah, he left her a little note in her drawer."

"What are we going to do with you?" Luca says.

"Let him go."

"Are you serious?"

"Yes, I'm sure he's going to run to his lackey and tell him that he failed to get his target, but if he ever comes near my woman again, I'll chop off his balls and serve them to his wife in a nice bolognese." Luca took the rest of the vial and blew it in the officer's face before taking the cop's hand and helping him empty his gun clip but leaving the one round in the chamber. We don't want him to get a couple shots off at us.

"Switch cars. I want to use your trunk," I tell Luca.

"I don't want her clawing up my shit like she did your face," he gripes like a big-ass baby, but I do have to say my fucking face stings like a motherfucker.

"I have the emergency blankets in the Rover. Load them nicely in the back and come on. I don't want anyone seeing me carry her like this." I toss water on her face before we leave the apartment, and she hisses at me. Fuck, she's like a feisty cat.

Luca gives me a disapproving look, but it's only because he's afraid of his trunk getting fucked up. I'll pay for the repair if it does. My woman is a bit rough around the edges, and it only makes me love her even more. I thought she would be my opposite, but I'm learning we are very much alike.

"See ya later, Officer Nick. Just remember that I'll report you if anything happens to my woman. In fact, I think I'll report you anyway," I say, walking out of the apartment with my woman's ankles and wrists zip tied.

Tossing my sweet woman in the car while she lunges at me like a demented kitty, I do my best not to chuckle at how cute she looks. I do feel awful for having to tie her up, but what am I supposed to do? She would have harmed herself. The drive is a short one and with the lack of traffic, it will be even shorter.

A loud bang comes from inside the building, taking us by surprise. It's the sound of a gunshot. Strange. It was too sudden for us to see if there was a muzzle flash, but I can already guess which apartment it came from.

CHAPTER SIX

JANUARY

A BUMP IN THE ROAD SHOCKS ME AWAKE FROM this hazy, strange state, and I find myself in a dark space. The sound of the engine revving and the steady movement told me all I needed to know. I was locked in a trunk. Did Jason find me? Panic sets in quickly and I start shouting, banging around. "Let me out."

"Calm down," comes a muffled voice. It takes me a moment to recognize it as Enrico's.

This motherfucking asshole. He's going to pay for tossing me in the trunk. I can't even believe he did that. I was only teasing about running away, but the damn man took me at my word. Now, the prick has me bundled up in a cushioned trunk that smells too clean.

Really? I'm not going to punch him in the balls. No, I'm going to find another way to make him pay. I wonder what

I can do. All I know is he's asking for it, and I'm sure as fuck going to give it to him. I hiss and shout, hoping someone hears me. He's stopped and talking to someone so damn calmly as if he doesn't have me in the trunk.

I'm going to kill him when I get out of the confined darkness.

"Let me out, you fucking asshole," I shout again, hoping whoever he's speaking to can hear me and are willing to help me. Unfortunately, they're useless because he starts driving away from those pricks. They're probably one of the many thugs that work with him and so I'm just screwed.

The vehicle comes to a complete stop, and then he has the nerve to say, "Time to let the terror out." The terror? I'm the terror? He's my freaking kidnapper if he has forgotten.

As soon as he opens the trunk, I'm on him like a rabid damn animal. "Asshole." I bang on his chest, but he quickly grabs my wrists, stopping my assault.

"Fuck, not again, baby girl," he groans, slamming his eyes closed and letting out a sigh.

Again? He kidnapped me twice, so he has a lot of nerve. I stare at him in disbelief at his audacity. That's when I see his face. "What happened to you?" He looks like he's been mauled by a cat.

He cups my face and then presses the back of his hand on my forehead, checking my temperature. "I'm fine, but I don't know how I ended up in the trunk."

"Sweetheart, you don't remember it, but let's just say we had a little problem with your landlord's cop buddy."

It comes back to me. We stopped back at the apartment to find a cop rummaging through our things. We were about to leave when I can't remember anything except that I was scared. "Oh my God—I did this to you, didn't I?"

"Yes. He blew some fucking ketamine in your face. You were tripping. I had to dump you in the trunk so you didn't scratch me anymore." How damn strong was that drug? When I look at Enrico, I feel like a fool. I attacked him.

"I'm so sorry," I whisper, laying my head on his chest.

He gently caresses my shoulders and then "It's okay, baby. The doctor's already here, waiting to see you." He takes my legs and wraps them around his waist, and I feel terribly guilty about the cuts on his face, so I brush my lips along his ruddy cheeks.

"I'm so sorry." My eyes well up with tears as I brush my hands and lips over his neck and face.

He swats my bottom. "Relax. You've already got me hard as hell with your tight little body against mine."

"Oh, oops." I hide my face as I giggle.

"Don't apologize again. Just relax. I need you to be taken care of before you hurt yourself or before I fucking forget my manners and fuck you against the side of the damn house. You don't need to add brick burns to your injuries."

"Do you really have any manners?" I teased.

"You know, only June thinks I'm nice." My stomach just did a flip and not in a good way. I want to remain objective, but June's my friend and if he wanted her...I don't know how to handle that emotion.

"You've hung out with June?" My tone is harsh. I can't hide my jealousy and it's stupid, but it's sitting at the top of my throat and beating in my heart.

He chuckles and shakes his head. "Calm down, my fiery princess. June works for Dario as well, so she and I have met several times. I have no interest in her. You're the only one I want, so no need for the claws."

"I'm not jealous," I lie badly.

"Don't bullshit me. You've got nothing to worry about. Now behave before I show you that you're my only one."

He takes me into a smaller house than the mansion we just passed by, but it's gorgeous. I could get used to living here as long as it's with Enrico. "Welcome home," he whispers against my ear, kissing my throat as I tilt my head to give him room.

We're interrupted by his phone vibrating in his pocket. He pulls away to check it and then he lets out a chuckle.

"What's going on?" I asked, feeling so unsure.

"It's from Alessio. It seems I'm not the only one who is in trouble for putting you in the trunk. June isn't happy with him." I giggle and shake my head.

"Oh yeah?" I wonder what they're saying, but he doesn't leave me waiting long.

"Sure, look at the text." *Don't hurt January or my woman won't be happy.*

He types out a message and then lets me see it. *I don't hurt women. Even if she's a sexy brat.*

Alessio sends a quick response. *Bribe her with the kittens. She loves kittens too.*

She might toss one of them at me, Enrico sends back.

She'd never hurt them. That has to be one of the girls. "June is responding now," I say with a grin.

Good idea.

Talk to your woman, not mine. Alessio. I have to laugh because he's jealous too.

Enrico ensnares me in his grasp, hugging me with my back to his chest. "He's crazy. I only want to talk to you anyway. June's nice and all, but I never understood why they were wasting their time with women until you popped up in my life."

I spin around in his arms and scoff, "Popped up? I believe you hunted me down."

"Technically you popped out of a window and straight into my arms." He has me there.

A knock at the front door causes him to leave me for a moment and then an elderly man enters, taking a look between the both of us. "Shit, you look more worse for wear than she does."

I blush, shame filling me for having attacked him in the first place. He shakes his head and takes my hand in his, bringing it to his lips as he takes a seat beside me. "Take care of her. We believe she had ketamine blown in her face."

"Okay. Well, we can do some bloodwork, but if she's not feeling high or unwell, she'll be just fine. It will run out of the system pretty quickly."

"Thanks. I just need her to be okay." My heart melts. Enrico doesn't seem like the type to be so sweet, but this dangerous man is adorable.

"And you need some of those cuts to be taken care of before they become infected," I insist.

"Fine. For you, I will."

"Good. I don't want to leave you with any more scars." I run my hand over the scar I noticed when we met. Although I find that one sexy, I don't want to be the one who gave him more scars.

"Oh. That one I got as a little boy, jumping off a tree." Wow, I can just imagine him being a wild boy acting brutish and running into trouble even then. "I didn't learn my lesson well back in those days."

"I'm sorry about your face."

"It's okay. I should have done a better job of protecting you. You're my sole purpose in life now." I brush my lips against his and he groans, feeling the burn.

"Oops." I pull back, but he just cups my face and drags me in for a deeper kiss.

It's not long until the doctor leaves after taking care of both of us and Enrico says, "How about we go lie down?"

"I'd like that, but first can we shower? I want to rinse off my apartment. I feel icky. Besides, someone threw me in a trunk that probably had other bodies in it before. It's gross."

"Oh, hell, no. Don't let Luca hear you say that. He loves his vehicles and wouldn't ever do that. You were the first. I assure you he wasn't pleased with the switch this morning."

"I was the first person dumped in his trunk? I feel so special."

"By me," Enrico growled. Is he actually jealous? I try not to smile too much, but his attitude arouses me.

"Look. You have almost all my firsts, so relax. Now—are you going to take me to the shower, or are you going to sit there looking grumpy all day?" He scoops me up and rushes me upstairs where the shower is useless because we get filthy all over again.

WHEN WE WOKE UP I NOTICED THAT HE HAS another scar on his chest, but this one is larger than the one on his chin. I saw it the other day, but I never asked. Things were messy then, but now, I know where I belong and I don't want to leave Enrico's side, ever.

I sit up, resting my upper body on my elbow while my hand presses just below his scar. "Rico, what happened here?"

He places his hand over mine and then stares into my eyes. "Amore, that's from the night my nonno was murdered."

"What?" I can't fathom what he'd been through. "Oh my goodness. Murdered?"

"I visited my nonno every summer in Italy. One summer, a local group of thugs were breaking into homes, robbing to gain their reputation. They came into ours and my nonno was asleep in the living room as usual in front of the television. I was in my room, reading when I heard the commotion. They beat him and stabbed him. When I came out they slit me with a knife across the chest and ran." He pauses, the pain of the memory too great.

Enrico's eyes slam shut, shaking his head from side to side as the past haunts him. I feel guilty for even mentioning it now. I love this man.

I brush the scar with my hand, caressing it before I place a kiss on it.

He lifts my head and kisses my lips. "I was only twelve years old at the time, so I didn't have the strength I have now to fight back, but I eventually got my revenge. From that day, I became a different man. The man you see before you." I can see the rage simmering at the surface.

"I love the man you are, raging beast and all."

He flips me onto my back, kissing me roughly with his hands in my hair. He gently breaks our kiss, and then whispers, "I love you, January."

I can't believe this big brute is mine and I have no intention of running away from a love that only he can give me.

CHAPTER SEVEN

ENRICO

"HAVE A DRINK AND CALM YOUR ASS DOWN," Alessio says, handing me a rocks glass. I take it from him and let the cool liquid pour down my throat.

"Damn, one is all you need. We don't need you hunting down Strongman tonight," Dario says.

"I know what I have to do and what I want to do. They're not the same fucking thing which sucks. For as long as I've worked for you, I've never given you a reason to have you question my behavior."

"Yes, but this is different and you know it. January means everything to you and a slight against her deserves retribution." I nod.

"And in due time, I will have it one way or another, but...I have to get her new clothes like yesterday, but the matters with Thompson and Strongman have to be dealt with quickly. I can't say if there is anyone else, but there could be," I explained to the guys as I paced Dario's office, raking my fingers through my hair. Protecting January is my sole preoccupation.

"Leave the clothes up to Mrs. Ricci and the girls. They're all huddled together cursing us out upstairs as we speak," Dario says. I brought January over to the main house on the estate this morning because the important matters needed to be discussed.

"There's no need to handle Thompson. It seems he accidentally offed himself," Luca says, walking into the room with a cup of coffee and not a care in the world.

"What?"

"You remember the bang when we left?" Luca says.

I nod. "Yes, but I thought he shot it off into a wall or some shit."

He shakes his head and smirks.

"Nah, the dumb fuck was too high. The contact I have in the police department mentioned that it was an accidental discharge since they found the open ketamine vial next to him. Apparently, he wasn't even supposed to be on duty or at the apartment. He was under investigation since he often dined at Coleman's diner."

"Good. So they think he ransacked the place?" Dario asks, verifying the details.

"Yes. It looks like it, or at least what they believe is he must have tripped in the darkness, busted his mouth, and spilled his vial. In his stoned state, he killed himself, or maybe he intentionally killed himself when he couldn't find what he was looking for. They don't know, but the wound was self-inflicted."

"Damn—good. Now we have one to go," Alessio says, rubbing his hands together.

"Also lunch is ready."

We exit his office to go looking for our women to have lunch and then we'll figure out a plan to deal with the rest of the assholes.

"Fellas," January calls out from the staircase, looking too hot for her own good and every damn male around. I growl, seeing her in a sexy business-dress pant suit. What the fuck is she doing in that?

"What are you wearing?" I growl, eyeing her from head to toe.

She pops down the last step and saunters over to me in a pair of killer heels that add to her sex appeal. I want to strip her bare and have those fuckers cup my fucking ears while I drill into her tight pussy, breeding her cunt. "I have to go back to the office tomorrow."

"The hell you do," I snarl, dragging her to my side, slamming my mouth onto hers to silence that stupid shit falling from it.

"Actually..." Dario interjects. I pull back and snarl at my boss.

She smiles at Dario and now I get why Alessio was so damn jealous. "See, I was thinking that since Jackass Jason doesn't believe I'm onto him, and like I just overheard—"

"Fucking snooping again. She's definitely a reporter," I tease. She nudges me in the ribs. "A dirty shot," I grumble.

"Whatever." She rolls her eyes at me. "Anyway, as I was saying, I could stroll in, roll with whatever lie he tosses out, and make my presence known. It will make him nervous, and of course he can't react in a public place. I'll be able to gather what I need to bury him when I'm there while also bowing out of the position properly. I don't want the police wondering why I just disappeared."

"Great idea. We could really use her," Dario says, pointing at her while smiling with pride. I'd be jealous if he wasn't madly in love with his wife.

"I don't like it," I grumble anyway because it's total bullshit to put my woman in danger.

January places her soft hand on my chest, rubbing it up and down, getting me hard in a split second and right now, I'll agree to fucking anything. "You can wait for me if you like," she says in a sweet voice that goes straight to my balls.

"You know damn well I will because there's no way in hell I'm going to leave you unprotected." I cup her face, cradling her beauty in my hands, knowing I could never live without this woman and tomorrow is going to kill me.

"We're going to head out now. Get your shit because I need to spank your ass for putting yourself in danger."

"I haven't yet."

"But you set it for tomorrow. Brains and booty. I'm going to fuck the hell out of you all through the night."

Several hours later, we finally come up for air and I'm still unhappy with the idea of her going into the office with Jason being there. It's not safe as far as I'm concerned because I don't know who he has working for him. It might just be the four fuckers, but when you run a trafficking ring, it's not just the main guys. They have buyers, handlers, and middlemen along the way.

I toss the covers off and climb out of the bed.

"What's wrong?" January sits up in bed, placing the sheet over her ample tits. Damn, I could tug that fucker off right now and push her back down, fuck the stress out right now between her thighs, but I know she's going to be too damn sore.

"I need to work out," I grumble.

"You don't call that a workout?" she says, sounding bewildered, sweat still on both our bodies. I know I'm being unfair to her, but I'm not used to this. I've been alone my entire life, and now she's here and things are different.

"I need a different kind of workout."

"Okay. Do you have anything to eat? I'm kind of hungry." Shit. I forgot to feed us in my urge to get her home and fuck her. "Don't look so distraught. It's okay. I can wait."

"No, there's food. I just forgot to make you something."

"Relax. Just point me in the right direction, and get that aggression out while I get some food." She jumps out of bed, losing the sheet, and her tits bounce in my face. I scoop her up, sucking one of those fat suckers in my mouth. "Let's go." I walk with my mouth latched to her chest.

Once we get to the kitchen, I finally release her, setting her down on her feet. "Sweetheart, having you naked in the kitchen is a dream come true."

"I just better be careful not to fry anything," she teases. I slip off my shirt and slide it onto her body.

"That should help. I'll be back in a little while." I kiss her once more and head down to my gym and go a few rounds to destress.

Flavio has been working around the clock on this, but I don't like sitting on my thumbs. After my sweaty workout, I run up the stairs and check on January, but she's no longer in the kitchen.

So, I head into my office and give Flavio a call from my desk office. It takes forever for him to answer. "Son of bitch. What took you so long to answer?"

"It's only two in the morning." Fuck. I took off my watch and didn't even bother to look at the time. "Some of us average humans actually sleep, you know," he grumbles.

"Sorry. I wanted to know what you got on Strongman."

"He's got a small network of street hustlers and pimps. They don't know him since most of the people were associated with Thompson and Johnson. They were the messengers. Strongman looks to be the shadow man. No one sees him, and he has no ties other than the connection to Ms. Holmes and the cop, which we realized when you went after him the other day."

"Damn, I need a way to get to him. We need a way to tie him to the trafficking without getting our hands dirty." We can't afford to be implicated in Johnson's death, although right now, it's looking like Coleman's the killer.

"I say we need someone at his station to rat him out, or maybe someone close to him who knows his whereabouts." Damn it, so far it looks like everything leads to my woman going back into the lion's den.

"Fine. Well, everything is underway for that. Goodnight." I end the call and find January by the door, leaning on it. "I wondered where you were."

"I went to bed, thinking maybe you'd come join me, but it's not looking like you want to sleep tonight." She seems sad and I know that it's my fault somehow.

"I'm coming up right now, but I have to rinse off."

"You must have had a lot of stress to unleash."

I brush my fingers under her chin. "Some of it I took out on your sweet pussy, but I don't think your cunt could handle the darkness I had left in me."

She smirks and then raises her eyebrow with attitude. "Why? Do you think I'm weak, Mr. Barone?"

"No, I just don't want to be too rough with you."

"Says the man who tied me up and threw me in the trunk of a car."

"I think you have a point. Besides, I believe you're tough enough to deal with my rage."

"Show me, my brute."

I rush around the desk, grab her around the throat, throw her across the surface, pinning her there with my chest over her back and holding her down. "Do you still want me to show you how crazy I am when it comes to you?"

"Yes," she moans, and the vibration in my hand only spurs on the pure lust. I free myself from my shorts and lift her shirt up to see she hasn't bothered to put on any panties.

"You were just waiting for me, keeping this pussy open for me to take." I slap her ass hard. "So fucking good. The thought of losing you is unbearable. Stop me if this is too much."

"Please don't stop. Fuck me, brute. Show me how much you want to tear my pussy apart. Punish me for putting my nose in your business." I take her breathy command as word and stuff my fat cock into her sopping wet entrance, stealing her breath as I push in deep, rattling my desk.

"Fuck. You're going to make me come fast." My hands move down, plucking on her round tits that will be growing bigger soon because I haven't used any fucking protection. I'm going to be adding to the group of kids around here. Although, I'm not sure I'll be a good father. I'm a terror, but I'm sure as hell a great protector.

"I'm coming with you," she moans out.

"Fuck, you're going to make me fill you with my sons."

"Or daughters," she challenges, knowing that will irritate me. Princesses are too much trouble and one like her will be dangerous.

"Not if I can help it," I roar, strumming her clit and sending us both over the edge.

"You know you can't control that."

I pull out and kiss her flat belly. "The hell I can't. The way I just screwed you, there's no way an angel can be born from that. My little Satan was created in mommy's womb."

"Or you can have a hell's angel."

"Then we'll all need help." I pull her into my arms and kiss her while gripping the back of her neck. I tilted her head upward and checked her for bruising. There's nothing there, but I'm a big motherfucker and I'd hate myself if I ever hurt her.

"I'm fine. I'm more than fine. As a matter of fact, I'm completely satisfied, so how about we get some sleep since I have a really big day in a few hours?" Did she have to remind me about that? It's like she's asking for her pussy to be perpetually destroyed.

"Okay," I grunt, carrying her to our bed. Finally, we close our eyes around three in the morning, but my sleep is fitful as I consider all the ways I want to destroy Strongman and the ways he could hurt my January before I can get to her.

CHAPTER EIGHT

JANUARY

AFTER A QUICK DEBRIEFING WITH DARIO THIS morning, I stepped into the lobby of the station, pretending that nothing's wrong. I'm running on hardly any sleep frayed nerves, but I have to do this, though. Smiling at security, he greets me and is surprised to see me. "Good morning, Ms. Holmes."

"Good morning, Tony," I say sweetly. Technically, we were supposed to be gone for another couple of days, but with the story falling through there was no point in staying away.

I walk past him and that's when I spot Marion. The show's producer comes up to me. "Oh, it's so good to see you." She wraps me up in a hug.

"Good morning, Marion," I say, giving my best attempt at normalcy.

"I wasn't sure I'd see you in today given all the stuff with your landlord." It's been all over the news, so I'm sure she's been made aware of it, but is that what Jason told her about our trip? I need to dig a little deeper.

"Yeah, I was able to make it in. Didn't want to completely let you guys down. Where's Jason?"

"He's in the middle of a call, but the staff meeting is in ten. I'm sorry about your landlord. I heard the police required you to return to Chicago, calling the project short." I nod, shaking my head and absorbing her sympathy with just the right amount of sadness.

"Yes, so sorry about it all as well. It's a real loss to the station since the scoop was a bust." So that's the story Jason spun about my sudden departure from the cabin. Good. I'm glad I didn't have to lie. Holding my head up high, I walk into the conference room and take a seat in my usual spot just beside Jason's chair.

He walks in, stutter steps and turns pale, but after he regains his composure, he takes a seat next to me. I lean in and whisper. "I've agreed with your story. It's better than mine."

He nods and then focuses on the paper in front of him. I watch as his Adam's apple bobs rapidly, and I do my best not to laugh. When I first walked in, I was petrified, but now, I'm cool, calm, and collected because I'm the one with the upper hand while he's on edge.

Our staff meeting goes on for an hour as the producers go over the schedule and the headlines that are up for discussion for the next day and the two exposés that will run at the end of the week. We never finished ours, so it's on the back burner, but I don't care because today's my last day here. I'm going to the producer's office to tell her that after the meeting.

The purpose of coming here was to give Jason a little scare. I'm sure Enrico's probably not pleased with me even though he let it happen. I didn't want Jason spreading lies and getting the police after Enrico or the rest of the Conti Family. Dario and the others saw the validity of my proposal, and if I hadn't been who I am, Enrico would have as well.

"Marion, can we have a chat?"

"Sure, but it's going to have to wait a bit longer, okay?" I nod and go about my day. When I go for my usual caffeine fix, I run into Jason getting his own.

Jason approaches me and says, "If I were you, I'd just leave without another word. It's for the best."

"I'm sorry. Are you threatening me?" I questioned, ready to call for Enrico.

"I'm giving you a friendly warning." He pulls out the stirrer from his coffee cup and drops it into the trash before leaving the room. My brow raises up as I stare at the back of him even after he disappears from my line of sight. Shit. What does he mean by that? I really need to get out of here.

I make it through the morning and then midafternoon when Marion finally calls me into her office. "I'm so glad you could come into my office. I know you had a rough experience with Jason. Things with him can be difficult…if you know what I mean."

I squint, wondering if she is talking about his activities or just the general egotistical bastard he is. "I'm sorry. I don't."

"Don't play dumb with me, January. You can lie to everyone else, but I know everything about Jason."

"Okay, so I don't know what you think you know, but…I had to go back home."

"You would have been a great asset. You could still do well." I don't think she's talking about the news station anymore. I pressed the panic button in my bracelet that they fitted me with before I left the house. It not only alerts them to my whereabouts but also records about ten minutes of conversation. Hopefully it won't last that long because Enrico and several others will make their way through here to get me at any moment.

"I'm sorry, but I'm not interested in working for the station anymore. I've been through a lot lately."

"Is it because of the death threat?" she asks. Death threat? The only one I got was in…my underwear drawer.

"How…" Before I can finish my sentence, she's on her feet with a gun in my face.

The look on her face has shifted. Gone is the sweet, kind older woman and in its place is an old hag, something out of an evil fairy tale. Her wrinkles are more prominent, the rage in her eyes visible and vibrant. "Get up and follow me out like a good girl, January, and there won't be any problems."

"What are you talking about, Marion? Why are you doing this?" I stand with my hands up in the air.

"Put your fucking hands down, you look stupid." I follow her directive, but I bet it's just to make her look less suspicious as we leave. Still, I need to find a way, to get some distance because this bitch is crazy.

"Marion, I don't get it. Why are you doing this?"

"You weren't supposed to make it through the weekend with Strongman, but fucking Coleman couldn't control his temper with Johnson. I knew it wouldn't be long until one of them killed the other, but then you had to run from Jason. He was my damn scapegoat. A man with too much ego and bravado who could take the fall when an innocent intern disappears or quits and too many questions get asked. If you hadn't run away, I would have gotten you away from him by the end of the next day while he was interviewing the contact."

"There never was an assignment there, was it?"

"So you were all working together? Coleman, Johnson, the cop Nick, Jason, and yourself?"

"No. Jason was working on a story, or so he believed. Soon, it won't matter. The horn dog will take the fall for everything. Now get moving before I blow your brains out and say you came after me because I fired you." I can't believe this. Madam Marion here was the fucking ringleader.

I nod and move toward the door, anxiously waiting to create some distance. "Don't even think of alerting anyone. I'm not afraid of shooting up this place. There are a lot of cops on my side."

"Please. I won't tell anyone. I just want to go home, and that's it. No trouble, I promise."

"Bullshit. The second we get out of here, you'll call the cops." I shake my head. On the contrary. I'd never get the cops involved if I could help it because of Enrico. "Let's go."

We move down the hallway to the elevator. She jabs it impatiently, seriously freaking ten times in a row. "It's not going to come any faster."

"Shut the fuck up."

"Why should I? You're already threatening me and everything." The light turns off on the button, and panic fills me. Shit, where the hell is Enrico?

Just then, the elevator doors open and my brute looks right at me. Most wouldn't be able to read him, but I know everything about my man and even under the shadow of darkness hidden in his nature the love and concern is there for me.

I dart just my eyes her way, and he understands. Enrico and Luca step out first, and then as she reaches to nudge me inside, Enrico grabs my wrist, dragging me away and Luca whips the producer around, slamming her against the wall.

"Security," someone shouts.

"Good. Call them," Enrico calls out.

"Did you get it all recorded?" Luca asks.

"Yep." I press the button and it plays back. A crowd forms around us, and Jason stares on.

"You son of a bitch," my brute shouts.

"No, leave him alone." He looks at me like I've lost my mind, but then we're taken into a room when the cops arrive, and in about twenty minutes the conversation is replayed and Marion Webber is arrested for kidnapping, attempted felonious assault, and numerous other charges. They are working on her other charges, but it makes me feel better that the real danger has been dealt with.

"So what the hell am I supposed to do with Strongman?" Enrico roars.

"He's a fucking pervert who wanted to seduce your girl, but other than that, he's nothing more, so there isn't much left to do. There's no guarantee that he wouldn't have assaulted her, but he hasn't before. Yes, he's used his power to influence women to sleep with him."

"So he's a piece of crap, but he's not like the others."

"I'm sorry, my friend, but it's not like we can kill him now. We have eyes on us because of everything that's happened," Luca says.

Enrico isn't happy about that idea, but I am. As much as I love my brute, the thought of having him locked away for life doesn't sit well with me, and Jason Strongman just draws too much attention for the cops not to notice.

"Now that that is all over, can we go home? Because I'm worn out."

"Princess, you haven't begun to see worn out. I'm not done with you yet," he growls. The warning changes everything in me. Suddenly, I have all the energy in the world. Smiling from ear to ear, the ride home to the estate seems to take forever.

CHAPTER NINE

ENRICO

THE PRIEST JUST LEFT AND AS WE WAVED HIM off, I'm trying to control my excitement. I'm married to January. It had been the happiest day of my life because now I had her tied to me. All we needed to do was get started on our family. Although I'm sure I've been putting in the work to make that happen.

I grin when I remember what happened this morning. She looked so damn delectable in her sexy underwear that I was meant to tear off after we said, "I do." Still, I couldn't wait, and I snuck into her room, peeling the lacy material off her smooth, pale skin while I ate her out for breakfast.

"What's on your mind, husband?" The sound of my new title only adds to the blood flow south. It's like a dam broke and I'm stiffer than a board. I reach out and take her hand, placing it on my aching shaft. "Yeah, that doesn't help. For all I know you're thinking about murdering someone."

I chuckled, cuffing her wrist and pulling her around to face me. "Wife, all I'm thinking about is how hot this morning was. This arousal is strictly for you." I plant my lips on hers, sliding one hand into her long red hair as I tasted her.

She pulls her face away first, panting as she stares into my eyes. "If you thought this morning was hot, you should see what I'm wearing underneath this dress now." I growl and scoop her up, carrying her over my shoulder into the house and away from our guests. Luckily, it was just Alessio, Luca, Dario, and both May and June.

The entire party laughs. "Have a good night," Dario says.

"We will," January blurts out over my shoulder, waving goodbye.

An hour later I had a message from Dario. He let me know that they cleared the food and then left, locking up on their way out.

"Everyone left us," I informed my wife.

"Oops, they know what we're doing." She blushes and I let out a belly-deep laugh.

"Are you serious? I thought you knew that before."

"I mean, I did, but it's just hitting me that we left our mini-reception to have sex." I can't stop chuckling because she actually looks embarrassed.

"Stop. It's not funny. What are they going to think of me?"

"Are you serious? Other than Luca, I'm sure the rest of our guests were going home to fuck. All they're thinking about is how I couldn't wait to consummate our marriage." I wag my brows and tickle her sides.

The more she laughs, the less embarrassed she was. So I continued until she pleaded for me to stop. "Enough, he… he…oh goodness. I can't breathe," she gasps, smiling at me as I bend down and taste her lips.

"I'm sorry, but God, January." I growl. "You look so damn sexy right now."

"Just right now?" Damn that reporter picks up on every word or action. I'm going to have to be careful the way I word things.

"Always, but there's a beautiful flush that's spread across your cheeks and your eyes are bright. You're so damn hot," I confessed, nipping at her neck and down to her shoulder.

"Thank you. You're pretty damn sexy yourself." She runs her fingers through my hair and then caresses my jaw.

"What would you like to do with the rest of our evening, Mrs. Barone?"

"First, I need a bath and then you need to feed me, Mr. Barone."

"Take a bath shower alone, so we don't end up back in bed while I shower in another room."

"Sounds like a smart idea, husband." Damn, is she trying to make me stay. "Don't look at me like that. I can't help calling you that."

"Well, it's going to get you fucked again, so hold off until you want that pussy tore up."

"Now, you're not helping. Get out, Enrico." She shoos me away as she enters our bathroom. I take loose fitting pajama pants, and a pair of boxer briefs before making a dash out of our room into one of the guest bedrooms.

Luckily all of them are filled with towels and soap just in case we have company. I'm quick with my shower because I can't wait to feed her, so we can continue where we left off.

As I exited the guest bathroom with just a towel around my waist, I stared at the bedroom and wondered if this would be our child's room one day. It's too early to know if I knocked her up, but it strikes me that I can't wait for this baby to come. I look forward to the day she tells me she's pregnant with our baby.

"Hey, what are you doing in here?" January steps into the bedroom and wraps her arms around my waist, resting her head on my chest.

"I was just thinking about our future family."

"Do you want kids?"

"Yes, I have been actively trying to fill your belly with our first baby."

"Well, I hope I'm a good mother."

"I'm sure you'll be great. Don't let those fucked up parents of yours stress you out. You're nothing like them."

"How would you know?" she asks, looking up at me and I can see she's on the verge of tears.

"Because you helped your friends, including June who was younger at the time. You showed that you're a great person and that frankly translates to a great mother. I'm sure you're going to spoil any little version of us that we have to prove you're not like your parents."

"You're right."

"But they will have to learn to be sneaky since you're a human lie detector. They won't get away with shit."

"That's good. I want them happy and safe," she smiles with pride.

"See, already you're getting ready for motherhood."

"Thank you, Enrico." Her stomach rumbles in my arms.

"Oh no, someone's hungry." She blushes ducking her head. I tip her chin to look at me once more before we go downstairs. "I think we both worked up an appetite,"

"Are you planning on putting any clothes, sir?"

"Oh shit, you got me so damn distracted. Give me five minutes."

"Don't take too long or it's going to look like a raccoon was in our kitchen. I'm feeling ravenous," she teases and pulls away. I'm left in the bedroom with just my thoughts which aren't happy ones. Her parents needed to feel the pain of their dismissal. I'll find some way to destroy a part of their lives even if I don't send them six feet down.

I hear pots and pans banging, so I quickly dress before she goes on a rampage. I step out of the bedroom and she's by the staircase with two pans, banging them together.

"Mrs. Barone, you're going to be a pain in my ass." I take the stairs two at the time and growl.

"Yes, as promised," she answers before turning on her heel and returning to the kitchen where I follow in a rush.

I'm never going to give up chasing this woman and her sassy ass.

CHAPTER TEN

ENRICO

IT'S BEEN A MONTH SINCE THE FUCKING incident at the news station. I haven't gotten to Strongman yet, but that's fine with me because I've planted the seed that will take care of the job for me. The right words whispered in the right ears. Soon he'll pay and I won't have to get my hands dirty.

There was no doubt in my mind that he planned on doing something to my woman, and I had the proof since he'd gotten footage from Johnson on my woman. The same video that sent me into a violent rage that night in Johnson's apartment. At least I won't have to do the dirty work. The little gift was delivered to Strongman's brother-in-law this morning who happens to be a big family man.

"Hey, you look proud of yourself," Dario says. His expression darkens. "Tell me you didn't get the fucker."

I roll my eyes and take a seat on his leather sofa in his office. "Of course I didn't. I told you that I wouldn't do it myself, but that doesn't mean his Colombian brother-in-law didn't need the information."

A devilish grin appears over his face. "Good work. That son of a bitch won't let that slide. He loves his sister and will destroy Strongman in a heartbeat when he gets the chance." We both learned that Strongman was a Colombian mob boss and took pride in family loyalty, so it was only a matter of time that our little problem would be wiped off the face of the earth.

"So did you know Strongman is doing a scoop in Colombia this week?" I added, adjusting the cuffs on my suit coat.

"That's interesting." We smirk and then he adds, "Are you ready for this evening?"

"I will be." We discussed my day of meetings. I had to coax a few of the people who owed us money into paying up. Luckily, I came back with a clean suit and a nice amount of money that Alessio set into the safe. I check the time on my watch and realize that I should have been home a while ago.

"We're good with everything. Let's call it now so we can make sure our women are ready for a special evening." My phone pings and I laugh. "What's up? Your wife up to something crazy?"

"No, I got my first revenge on her parents. It seems someone was skimming off the top at work. He's been fired."

"You're on a roll. You better be careful with your wife when you get home. I have a feeling she's going to get all of your excitement."

"You got that right." I grin, rubbing my hands together.

"Don't forget about tonight in the meantime," he warns me.

"It's time to go see my woman." I shook his hand and took my leave. Tonight is very special, so it's important to have January ready to go. As I drive back to the house, I wonder when we'll get the news that Strongman's missing and if it means he's gone for good. I'll have to talk to Dario about contacting the Columbian directly for verification. I'd hate for Strongman to talk his way out of his fate.

The smile that greets me when I enter the house takes away the tension in my bones. Her bright eyes have a mischievous glint to them that lets me know that she's either been up to no good, or she's about to be a bad girl.

I slide my arms around her slender waist, pulling her close. Our bodies touch and her sweet scent drives me wild. I'm tempted to just forgo all conversation and take her to bed, but I want to hear what mischief she has to share. "Tell me, princess. What am I supposed to do with you?"

"Just a kiss. I've been a very good girl. I missed you. Did you get the job done?" she asked me.

"Don't I always?" I tell her even though we have to wait for the results of my efforts.

She presses her hand to my chest, rubbing it. "It would seem so… I'm pregnant."

My eyes shoot wide open and I lift my woman up in the air, spinning her over my head. "Put me down before I get sick all over you."

I chuckle with untold happiness but remember to lower my beautiful woman to her feet without letting her go. "Sorry, baby girl."

"It's okay." She clamps her lips together to keep herself from getting sick and I mentally prepare myself for plenty of *it's okays* in the future.

"So are we telling everyone, or do they already know?" I ask my beautiful pregnant wife who is almost always attached to one of the girls.

She slaps my chest playfully while giving me the cutest damn pout. "I did the test by myself."

I threw my hands up and leaned back slightly. "Hey, you girls are close."

She dips her chin and sighs gently, placing a soft kiss on my chin. "Yes, but this is something I wanted just for us."

My heart swells at her consideration and love. "Good. Now it's time to celebrate you making me a daddy."

"I believe you made yourself a daddy. The rest is up to me and my doctors." I suppose she's right, but I couldn't do any of this without her.

"Well, you are the one who made me come, so you had a big part in that process too. Still, it's going to be my pleasure to spoil you along the way." I scoop her up in my arms and carry her off to our bedroom, remembering not to jostle her around. There are things we still need to discuss, but they can wait until I get her undressed and screaming my name.

There was something special I needed to do today, but I'd been so distracted by our news that I forgot. We made love again until we fell asleep.

My phone rings a couple hours later, and it's Alessio. "Fuck. What's up?"

"Have you forgotten?" he snarls into the phone. My eyes widened and I jump out of bed completely naked.

"Damn it. I did. We're on our way." I end the call in a rush and turn to January. "Sweetheart, I need you to get dressed as fast as possible. We need to be at the main house in ten minutes."

She drops the sheet from her sexy body, and I have to pull my gaze away because she's too damn perfect and a sensual distraction. "What's going on?" she asks, sliding off the bed.

"I can't discuss it."

Her right brow raises up and then she asks, "Is there anything I should be wearing?"

"I'd go with the new dress you got with May and June yesterday." She nods and runs into the closet. The guys and I have been planning this for a few weeks since we married our women, and I managed to screw it up.

About twenty minutes later, I arrive at the house with a breathtaking woman who doesn't have more than a swipe of lip gloss on her puffy kissed lips and is wearing a gorgeous green party dress. "You look stunning, January."

"Hardly." She blushes and I take my wife's hand, leading her into the backyard where everyone in the organization and a dozen friends and acquaintances have gathered to celebrate our nuptials.

Dario taps on his champagne flute with a spoon to address the crowd. "Welcome, everyone. On behalf of Alessio, Enrico, and myself, we'd like to introduce you to our beloved brides, June, January, and May. Thank you for coming here to celebrate in our joy. We are blessed to have found such insanely enchanting women who have stolen our hearts like the best thieves in the world."

Cheers erupt, and we're congratulated by many couples including a couple of other heads of crime families including Domani Bianchi who recently got married as well. His wife is now chatting with mine. "She will be fine. My wife is a sweetheart," I say when Bianchi watches their conversation.

"Forgive me. It's not your wife I'm concerned about. I don't take my wife's safety for granted. I nearly lost her, and I always remain close." I nod because it's a shared sentiment.

"That we can agree on."

"Hopefully, we can keep it peaceful for years to come." We shake hands and go to our women.

The moon and stars are out and bright tonight. They only add to the beautiful setup that Dario setup. All I can think about is taking my bride into my arms. So when we reach our ladies, I excuse us and pull January aside and head to the center of the dance floor to hold my wife closely for a special dance. "Thank you for not running away."

"Like you'd let me. I'd probably be zip tied and in a trunk again," she teases, pressing her hands on my chest.

"I'd even let you borrow my car again," Luca says, leaning in as he passes by us.

"Fuck off. Next time it will be my vehicle I toss her in," I reply, feeling territorial.

"I promise, Mr. Barone. There won't be a next time unless you're feeling a little kinky." She winks. I cup her ass in front of everyone because she has no idea how kinky she makes me. If I wasn't so territorial, I'd fuck her right on the dance floor under the summer stars.

"Fuck, I'm hard as hell," I growl against her ear. "It's too early to call it a night."

"Maybe we should find a room…" She rolls her hips, rubbing her hot pussy against my stiffening length.

I'll never get enough of this woman, and finding a room sounds like one hell of an idea. We sneak off to our guest bedroom and I lift up her dress, pulling down my pants far enough to stuff my huge cock in her soaking wet slit. Our orgasms hit us quick and we make it down to the party within fifteen minutes. Most don't notice we even disappeared, but the knowing look from Dario and May say they didn't miss our exit.

"It looks like you two are having a great night," he says.

"We are," January says with a big grin. "Thank you for hosting this celebration."

"It's my pleasure. We're practically family."

EPILOGUE

ENRICO

I QUIETLY CREEP THROUGH THE HOUSE FROM the secret entrance to avoid any of the kids seeing me covered in specks of blood when I'm instantly startled. I jumped back, almost pulling out my knife on the miniature version of my lovely wife with her eyes wide and her mouth parted.

"Daddy?" *Son of a bitch.* Vivian's slick butt spooked me.

"Angel, what are you doing down here?" I slide my knife completely back in place as my heart tries to come back down.

I'm grateful there's no real intruder in my home, but now I have a much bigger problem on my hands. She's too small to be in here and I can't tell how seeing me with blood is going to fuck her up in the head.

"Just waiting for you." She quirks up her lips and rocks on her heels with her hands behind her back, just like her mother when she's up to no damn good. The ringing in my ears hasn't stopped while my little sweet devil chatters on like she didn't just take a few years off her papa's life. "I love you and missed you, Daddy," she coos, smiling up at me with innocent eyes. If I didn't know better, I'd believe her, but she's too damn sneaky for her everyone's own good.

I knew a daughter would be trouble, but I thought it would be when she sprouted tits, and I had to go around chopping off anxious dicks after my little girl, but no, she started chaos early.

"You're supposed to be in bed, little Miss Vee," I gently scolded her and unlike other kids, especially around me, she doesn't look frightened.

She bites her bottom lip as she works on an excuse to be awake in her head. "Yes, well...why do you have blood on you?" she asks, too damn smart for her own good, and too inquisitive just like her mother. If she's like this now, I can't imagine when she's a teenager and tests our authority.

"That's none of your business, little one. It's time for bed, and I never want to catch you down here again." We've had all these kids and never once had any of them disobeyed me until she arrived. Since day one, my little hellion has shown me she's not taking shit from anyone including me.

My oldest, who was like me in many ways, quiet, tough, and gruff hadn't even tried to start this shit. Giovanni, who we named after my nonno had been a good boy. Even my second son, Marco, was no different. This one was conceived with sweet lovemaking and yet the devil came out.

"Okay, Daddy. You won't catch me." She smiles, and I know damn well I need to speak with January because our mini-one is a little too much like the both of us. Investigative like her mother and dangerous like me. I'm not sure if I'll have to keep her out of jail or from trying to work alongside me.

"Off to bed," I say, leading her out of the formerly secret area and back to her room. I don't tuck her in because I still need to wash up, but as punishment, I lock her bedroom door. Let the little damn terrorist find her way out. Although I shouldn't do it because by tomorrow morning Satan will have found a way and then she'll have learned a new skill.

Silently, I sneak into our bedroom where my beautiful wife lay asleep and I can't wait to slide in next to her, but I have to shower.

Still, I watch her for a moment because I can't get enough. All these years and she's everything to me. Finally I force myself away with the reminder that the sooner I finish with my shower, the sooner I can join her in bed.

It's hard to be quick and quiet in the water, but it doesn't matter because I hear her footsteps as she slides in behind me. "No matter how quiet you try to be, you can't get in without me knowing."

"I know, my love. I just don't want to disturb your sleep," I confessed.

"I missed you." She slides her hand over the front of my thigh, inches from my meat as water cascades down our bodies. Inhaling, I attempt to control the need to turn around and pin her against the wall.

"Wife, you're playing a very dangerous game right now. I'm in a fucked up mood." Horny and wired mixed with anxious rage.

"Yes, tell me about it, brute."

"The little hellion snuck into my secret entrance tonight and waited for me."

"Again?" she gasps.

"What? Again? What do you mean again?"

"I caught her the other night and watched her so she wouldn't do it again, but she's trouble."

"Damn it, you were a bad girl for not telling me. She scared the shit out of me. I almost pulled a knife out on her."

"Oh my God."

"Don't worry, your little devil knew just what she was playing at. Fucking five and evil as all can be." I shake my head because it's only going to get worse. I expected tutus and unicorns, but there isn't a horse with horns in her future, just a devil with horns.

"I don't know what we're going to do with her." January scoffs, letting out a suppressed giggle.

"Be careful," I whisper.

"Yes, very careful."

"But that doesn't explain your behavior, wife. You were a bad one." I grabbed her by the back of the neck, pulled her in close, placed my forehead against hers and stared into her beautiful eyes. "You should have told me that my little bad girl got into there before."

"What are you going to do?" There's a gleam in her eyes, knowing I'm going to fuck her hard.

"Knees now. You're going to please me until I'm sure you've learned your lesson." She rolls her eyes because there's no way in hell sucking my cock is going to teach her anything except she has me by the fucking balls.

She slides down and does unspeakable things to me until I come down her throat. I lift her up by her throat, and then pin her to the wall before dropping to my knees to eat her sopping wet cunt. Fuck, she's so delicious that I'm hard again in seconds. Flipping her to face the wall, I kick out her legs and slam into my wife from behind.

"Don't ever keep secrets from me," I growl against her ear as I take her hard.

"Yes, Rico." I love when she calls me Rico. It's rare and so worth it. That means I've hit the fucking spot she's needs, the hunger she's been craving. I pinch her clit and drive into her hole over and over until we're both shouting into the watery spray.

"You're a very bad girl." I fill her tight pussy with so much cum that it's going to be dripping out of her all night long.

"You made me this way."

"Little liar." She giggles. "You were feisty from the moment I met you."

"Except this time, I play nice with your balls."

"Yes, you do." I groan when she reaches down and rubs them so gently.

"Don't think this is over. I have the next couple of days of punishing you." I bite down on her shoulder and she lets out a moan. Who the fuck am I kidding? This will never be a punishment.

"I love you, January and this crazy family you've given me." Luckily, we only have one damn terror. The other two are pretty easy. Hopefully, they stay that way.

EPILOGUE

JANUARY

A DOZEN YEARS TOGETHER, AND I STARE AT MY husband in the middle of a family barbeque, hoping that he still finds me as interesting and attractive as I find him. The years have only made him hotter. I stopped being adventurous or daring after our last baby seven years ago. It's as if I changed completely from the young crazy girl he kidnapped all those years ago.

"What's wrong?" June asks, coming up to me holding her new kitten. Alessio would do anything for her, including adding a new pet to the house.

"Nothing," I mutter, sounding so damn unconvincing even to myself.

She purses her lips and shakes her head. "BS. Don't let Enrico see that look. He's not going to be pleased." I look for him and he's speaking with one of our female guards. A sense of sadness washed over me.

"He doesn't even notice me anymore," I mutter. He's spent half the party away from me. Yes, he's been playing with our kids and talking to Dario, but it's like I'm not even here.

"Girl, are you serious? Is something going on?" Honestly, I can't say. It's not like he doesn't make love to me, but I wonder if the family life is too much, or should I say I'm not enough anymore. My body hasn't changed much in the decade plus that we've been together, but I know I'm not young anymore and things don't stay where they belong anymore.

"I think I'm going to be a reporter again," I blurt out as I bend down to pet the kitten.

"Are you trying to get tied up again?" She giggles, knowing our husbands have made it clear that they're possessive, but I don't think that Enrico feels that way anymore. "I mean, it's a lot of fun, but he's probably going to go apeshit with men all around you all the time."

"What the fuck do you mean men around all the time?" Enrico's rich, deep voice growls darkly behind me. Uh-oh where the hell did he come from? I was just watching him from a distance.

Stiffening my shoulders, I turn around and face the handsome man I married a long time ago and say, "If you must know… I'm thinking of going back to reporting." I refuse to back down because my pain won't let me.

His face hardens and then he looks at June. "June, if you will excuse us and keep an eye on the kids for us?"

She smiles and winks before adding, "Sure, no problem."

Enrico grips my hands, pulling me away from everyone. With quick movements, my wrists are behind my back and my face is pressed against the rough exterior near the pool house. "If I must know?" he growls against the shell of my ear. "Who the fuck do you think I am? Since when do you think I don't give a damn what you're up to?"

"Why would you care? I'm older, plain, and...."

His hand comes down on my ass before I get to finish my next words. "Do you want to repeat that for me? I don't believe I heard that shit correctly."

"Enrico," I plead.

"Don't 'Enrico' me. No. You are so going to fucking get punished for that nonsense, wife." He frees himself from his shorts, pulls my sundress up, and thrusts into me from behind, finding his home deep in one stroke.

"You are mine, January Barone. No one else's and your place is at my motherfucking side, always." He deepens his penetration, shaking as he takes me violently, giving no fucks to who is around.

We fuck hard and fast against the wall with his hands roughly pinching and gripping my breasts, plucking my nipples. I'm unable to fight off my orgasm for long, and I bite my tongue to stop from screaming loudly as I come. His mouth latches onto my shoulder, biting down like a wild animal fighting his own roar.

"Fuck, January. I'm not going to lose you." He groans, spilling himself inside me. I freeze, wondering what that's about, stiffening in my spot.

"Lose me?" I push back, forcing him to move out of me and then turn around as he adjusts his pants. Gripping his cheeks, I stare at the man I'm madly in love with. "I don't know what's wrong with us."

"I didn't know anything was wrong with us." He stares at me so confused, pain in his eyes as if I just. "I'm sorry, my love. Please tell me what I did wrong."

"It's just... I'm not exciting anymore, and you're working with..." He started working with a female on the team and I can't take it. It's been bothering me more and more even though they don't actually work together at all. She's just one of many I can't help the pettiness in me.

"Is this about the damn movie I saw you watching the other day?" I hadn't thought about it, but I guess I let it get to my head.

"I don't know... Maybe."

"Sweetheart. Listen, I find you exciting by just existing. Every time I come home, it's a balm to my soul. For years I've done fucked-up shit and never cared about it and frankly still don't. I can do all that and not think twice, but I come home and I see you and that beautiful family you've given me, and it just makes me feel alive. You're the surprise I didn't know I wanted. You caught me off guard from the start, and even when you kicked me in the balls, I knew that you were going to be mine."

I let out the smallest giggle. "You're insane."

"That's a fucking given, but that doesn't change that I kidnapped you and made you mine, and I'm never letting you go. Remember, I fucking tossed you into the trunk once, woman. I'm not above showing that I'm keeping you any way I can."

"I have no intention of ever leaving you. I'm afraid you don't want me."

"Fuck, January. I'll always want you. That's a given, so enough with not being adventurous for me. Are you bored?"

"No, I'm happy with my life...too happy."

"Are you scared?"

"Maybe."

He wraps me up in his arms and holds me tightly. "January, when you were just becoming an adult and thought everything was good, your parents pulled the rug from right under you. Now you think I'll do that to you, right?"

"Maybe."

"I won't let you down. I love you and plan on expanding our little family."

"We've been married for ten years and have three children, one who is worse than both of us combined."

"Yes, but I think I just sealed it with baby number four."

"It doesn't work like that?"

"Well, I'm going to keep trying. If not, we have a wonderful life even if we have a little psycho on our hands."

EPILOGUE

HELLION'S EIGHTEEN BIRTHDAY

ENRICO

VIVIAN COMES RACING THROUGH THE FRONT door pissed as hell. A part of me doesn't blame her because she's a fucking boss in her own right, but she pushed the wrong motherfuckers buttons and she's lucky that he finds her fascinating. Matteo's reaction was well past rational, but as a man obsessed with his wife, I understood.

Of all my children, she's the only one to give me a hard time and the only one to give me gray hair.

"What's going on?" my beautiful wife looks at us in dismay which pisses me off even more than I already am, but I maintain control because this is a delicate matter.

"I hate him," she hisses. I don't know if she means me or Matteo. "I'm going to kill him. I don't care what anyone says. Capo or not." Matteo is her current enemy.

Well, she's always had an undercurrent of tension when it came to him. At first, she wanted to be a part of Dario's crew. When she was younger, we both shot that shit down because the thought of my daughter getting killed would have destroyed me and using her as a honeypot wasn't going to fly with any of us because she was growing into a beautiful woman like her mother.

Then as she got older her animosity for Matteo grew. I thought she wanted to be him, but January didn't believe so. She was under the impression that Vivian was trying to work out the normal romantic feelings that she was going through. Now, I know she's in love with Matteo even if she's confused by it.

"Who sweetheart?" January asks my hell's angel who is teetering on the edge of a knife between tears and violence. It's a woman thing that I learned a long time ago. They're so pissed that they want to cry from rage not sadness. It's not a fair fight for either of us because I hate for my wife to shed a single tear.

"Matteo," I say, coming into the room after her. Dario's eldest son and now the head of the Conti Crime Family since Dario retired this past week. The tension between them earlier was too much for me to witness. As a father, I wanted to punch him in the face, but as his enforcer and a man in love with his wife. I wanted to give him a handshake.

"What happened?" January asks again getting more and more anxious. I hate seeing my bride upset and my daughter knows it, so she looks at me with a new frustration as if this situation is all my fault.

Vivian throws her hands up. "He's an asshole is what he is and you're no better." She points right at me, shooting daggers. Matteo's got trouble on his hands. I don't need to give him shit because he's going to have to deal with my twisted daughter.

"Little girl, I'd watch it or you'll be in trouble," my wife scolds her, but there's no contrition on my daughter's face. She couldn't care less about anything right now.

"I'm already sentenced to a fate worse than death anyway, so whatever." She throws her hands up again, storming upstairs. I never expected overly dramatic to be a trait that Vivian possessed, but I suppose that's a new one. I'm not sure why she's upset about marrying Matteo, she didn't seem upset leaving his bedroom.

"Make sure she doesn't leave her room," I say to a few guards nearby. "And don't stand too close. She's feeling a bit testy and so is Matteo." They don't want to end up like the other bastard and I'm guessing Matteo isn't going to put up with any threat to his relationship with my daughter.

"What happened, damn it?" January hisses.

I slide my arm around her waist, knowing this is going to set her off and I'm going to get an earful. "They're getting married."

She leans back and glares at me. "Who? Vivian and Matteo?"

"Yes. Tomorrow."

"What? Why? No engagement?" She tries to pull out of my arms, but I hold her tight.

I run my hand through my salt and pepper hair with a heavy sigh. "Because he wants payment for her transgressions, and I think she'll finally learn how to behave before she ends up in prison or dead."

Resignation strikes her like it did me. We knew Vivian was going to be a handful, but now she'll be Matteo's problem. At least he loves her even though he wants to wring her neck like we do. I received his word that he'd never harm my baby girl and that's all I need.

"We're all in for a world of hell soon." She presses her head to my chest and sighs. "There goes the party for tonight."

"The hell it does," Matteo says, walking into our home uninvited. I'm still pissed about his actions with my baby girl, but if there's anyone who can tame that child it's him.

He's got a lot of his father in him and some of his grandfather as well. Crazy as fuck. "Where is my devil bride?" Matteo storms into our home without knocking.

"In her room, finding a way to escape," I say. "What brings you over here?"

"As expected. I came to make sure she's well-guarded. I have a feeling she's ready to do her usual escape tricks."

"You're calm about this," January says, eyeing him with suspicion.

"Well, I'm used to cleaning up after her, but she made me kill one of my capos today. A favorite and the brat did it on purpose, so if she wants the attention so badly, I'll give it to her, forever." I can't believe he killed his best friend over jealousy, something about what Vivian said didn't make sense. Flirting wasn't going to make Matteo lose his mind and kill someone he's known for fifteen years.

THE END

ABOUT THE AUTHOR

Find me on:

Website/Newsletter: www.cmsteele.com

Amazon Author Page: www.amazon.com/C-M-Steele/e/ B00MQ9FPZS/

Facebook: www.facebook.com/CMsteele2014

Instagram: https://www.instagram.com/c.m._steele/

Twitter: https://twitter.com/Author_CMSteele

Bookbub: https://www.bookbub.com/authors/c-m-steele

ALSO BY C.M. STEELE

A Best Friends Duet:

Picture Perfect * Instant Obsession

Best Friends Series:

Always You * His Dirty Secret * Sleep Tight

Bianchi Crime Family:

Married to the Mob * Captured by the Mob * Owned by the Mob

Cavanaugh Security Series:

Protecting Macy * Securing Blake

The Cline Brothers of Colorado:

Whatever it Takes * Taking Whatever He Wants * Finding
Paradise

The Conti Crime Family Series:

Alessio * Dario * Enrico * Matteo * Gio

Dirty Boss Series:

My Pet * My Cookie * My Flower * My Valentine

(Now on Audio)

The Falling Hard & Fast Series:

Falling for the Boss * Falling for the Enemy * Falling Hard

The Fiore Family:

Christmas with the Beast * Christmas with the Boss * Christmas
with the Sheriff

Gimme Series:

Sugar * Luck * Rain * Cream * Heat * Love

Say Something Series:

Say Uncle * Say Please * Say Uncle: Doggy Style

Second Generation:

Say Yes

Seasons of Love:

Wet Summer * Autumn Falls * Winter Frost

Sister Switch:

Testing Her Professor * Assisting Her Boss

A Steele Christmas:

Mason's Winter * Perfectly Wrapped * The Company You Keep

A Steele Fairy Tale:

My Gold * My Forever * My Property * My Prince Charming

A Steele Riders Family Novella Series:

Sammie * Roxie * Mike * Dylan

Steele Riders MC Series:

Boomer * Mick * Jackson * Doc * Beast * Ghost

Wrench * Blade * Boss * Cowboy * Law *Cyber

Steele Riders MC 2nd Generation Series:

Will * Julian

Southern Hospitality:

Down South * Gone South

Sweet Temptation Bay:

A Taste Of Honey * The Mayor's Surrender * Trapped with my Stalker

Sweetheart's Treats:

Sweet Surprise * Doctor's Orders, Sweetheart * Sweet Surrender

Twin Sin:

Stalk Me Please * Sinful Intent

White Wolf Ridge Series:

Turner

Wolfe Creek Series:

Wolfe's Den * Beta: Her Alpha

Raging Kane * Written in History

Standalones:

Auctioned to the Kingpin* Buying Love * Conquering Alexandria

Ecstasy Captured * Grant's Deal * In Heat * Intense

Killer Abs * Love Discovered * Loving My Neighbor * Lucky Ride

Mrs. Valentine * My Christmas Gift

Rainy Days * Stormy Nights * Red Hot Nights

Room Service * Scarred * Sharp Curves

So Wrong * Standing There

The Mobster's Virgin * The Wedding Guest * Unexpected

www.ingramcontent.com/pod-product-compliance
Lightning Source LLC
Chambersburg PA
CBHW020655260626
47157CB00008B/3046